JACKIE COLLINS

"The World is full of Married Men" is very special to me, ~~because it~~ is my first ~~book~~! Wow! Me, a school drop-out at fifteen, I never imagined in my wildest dreams ~~that~~ I would ever get my work published. But I had a dream, & I followed it, even ~~though~~ everyone said I was crazy, & ~~that~~ I would never get anything published.

But here I am, 28 New York Times bestsellers later, & still going strong! I am a true storyteller, and I like to think it shows. So please enjoy "The World is Full of Married Men", & always remember to follow your dreams.

Jackie C.

Praise for Jackie Collins

'Sex, power and intrigue – no one does it better than Jackie'

—heat

'A tantalising novel packed with power struggles, greed and sex. This is Collins at her finest'

—Closer

'Bold, brash, whiplash fast – with a cast of venal rich kids, this is classic Jackie Collins'

—Marie Claire

'Sex, money, power, murder, betrayal, true love – it's all here in vintage Collins style. Collins's plots are always a fabulously involved, intricate affair, and this does not disappoint'

—Daily Mail

'Her style is pure escapism, her heroine's strong and ambitious and her men, well, like the book, they'll keep you up all night!'

—Company

'A generation of women have learnt more about how to handle their men from Jackie's books than from any kind of manual… Jackie is very much her own person: a total one off'

—Daily Mail

'Jackie is still the queen of sexy stories. Perfect'

—OK!

'Cancel all engagements, take the phone off the hook and indulge yourself'

—Mirror

Also by Jackie Collins

The Power Trip
Married Lovers
Lovers & Players
Deadly Embrace
Hollywood Wives – The New Generation
Lethal Seduction
Thrill!
L.A. Connections – Power, Obsession, Murder,
Revenge
Hollywood Kids
American Star
Rock Star
Hollywood Husbands
Lovers & Gamblers
Hollywood Wives
The World Is Full Of Divorced Women
The Love Killers
Sinners
The Bitch
The Stud
Hollywood Divorces
THE SANTANGELO NOVELS
Goddess of Vengeance
Poor Little Bitch Girl
Drop Dead Beautiful
Dangerous Kiss
Vendetta: Lucky's Revenge
Lady Boss
Lucky
Chances

THE WORLD IS FULL OF MARRIED MEN

JACKIE COLLINS

ISBN number: 978-0-9857459-6-7 (paperback)
ISBN number: 978-0-9857459-5-0 (electronic book)

Library of Congress Cataloging in Publication
Collins, Jackie. World is Full of Married Men.
I. Title.
PZ4.C7112 Wo3 PR6053.O425 823/.9/14

eBook editions by eBooks by Barb for booknook.biz

Visit Jackie at her website **www.jackiecollins.com** and follow her on
Twitter: **@jackiejcollins**
Facebook: **facebook.com/jackiecollins**
Pinterest: **pinterest.com/jackiejcollins**

For Elsa with all my love

Chapter One

'When I was fifteen, I was amazing, absolutely amazing! Dear Mummy was terrified to let me out on my own, she felt I was bound to come home pregnant, or something silly like that.'

The speaker was Claudia Parker. The listener was David Cooper. Claudia was in bed. She was a very beautiful girl, and she knew it, and David knew it, so everyone was happy. She had long, shiny ash-blond hair, which fell thickly around her face, and a deep fringe down to her eyebrows, which accentuated her enormous, slanty green eyes. The face was perfect, with a small, straight nose and luscious, full lips. She wore no makeup and no clothes, and was covered by only a thin silk sheet.

David sat at the end of the bed. He was forty and looked it. He had black, slightly curly hair and a well-lined strong face. His nose was rather prominent, and he wore thick, horn-rimmed glasses. He was a masculine-looking man and enjoyed a great deal of success with the opposite sex.

'So eventually I left home,' continued Claudia. 'I mean it was just all too impossible and dreary. One night I sneaked out, never to return. Actually, I met this marvellous boy, an actor, and he brought me to London with him, where I've been ever since.' She sighed and wriggled around under the sheet. 'Got a cigarette, darling?'

David produced a packet of filter-tips from his dressing-gown pocket and handed one to her. She took a long drag. 'Want to hear more of my lurid background?'

'I want to hear everything about you.'

She smiled. 'You're so sweet. Not at all dull. I thought when I first saw you, you would turn out to be an absolute bore. But how wrong I was. I'm mad about you!' She leaned over to where he was sitting. The sheet was left behind as she wound her arms around his neck and started to nibble at his ear. She had a quite fabulous body.

He pushed her back on the bed.

'Want me, baby?' she whispered. 'Want me badly?'

He grunted his assent.

Suddenly she twisted herself free, jumped off the bed, and ran to the door. 'You're too much,' she said, 'but not now, darling. Maybe you can do it again so soon, but *I* need a little rest.' She giggled. 'I'm going to have a shower, then maybe we can get some lunch out; and then, baby, *then* we can come back and make it all night long!'

She vanished through the door, and David heard water running in the bathroom.

He thought about Claudia, and the way they had first met. Was it really only three weeks ago? He had had a particularly hard day at the office, and Linda, his wife, had been nagging him about all the extra work he seemed to be doing, and how she never saw him anymore. It was nearly six, and he was just getting ready to leave when Phillip Abbottson darted into his office.

'Listen, Dave,' Phillip said, 'do you have a spare moment to come down to the studio and make a decision for us? We've got two girls testing for the Beauty Maid soap product, and it's a dead heat. We just can't decide.'

Reluctantly David went with Phillip to the ground-floor studio in the enormous Cooper-Taylor advertising building. It was owned by his uncle, R. P. Cooper, who had two sons, and Sanford Taylor, with no sons but a son-in-law. Therefore, David came sixth in the line of importance, which in a business of such a size was quite important, but not important enough as far as David was concerned. He was in charge of the TV section, and since Beauty Maid soap was to be featured quite heavily on Channel 9, it was necessary to pick the right girl.

They entered the studio, and David immediately spotted her. She was sprawled in a canvas chair, wearing a white terry-cloth robe. Her hair was piled high on her head, and she was eating an apple. The other girl came into focus next. She was chocolate-box pretty, prim, and virginal-looking. However, her figure belied her face. She had a huge bosom, the largeness of which was emphasized by the flesh-coloured swimsuit she was wearing.

'What tits!' muttered Phillip.

'Is that all you ever think about?' said David.

Phillip called for silence in the small studio and gestured to the Chocolate Box girl. She made her way onto the small set, where a fake bathroom was located. She climbed daintily into a large, round marble bath, flesh-colour swimsuit and all, and a prop man rushed eagerly over and sprayed her ample proportions with bubbles. Someone else thrust a large

3

bar of soap into her hand, and then Phillip shouted, 'OK, let's do it.'

The cameras started to turn, and David watched the scene on a small closed-circuit screen.

The girl flashed a toothy smile at the camera. 'I'm a Beauty Maid,' she cooed. She lathered the soap in her hands and spread it luxuriously up her arms, first one, and then the other. 'Beauty Maid was made for me. It's so creamy, so smooth, so datable.' She drew one long leg out of the bubbles and lathered that too. 'Why don't you try Beauty Maid, and then you can be a Beauty Maid too!' She smiled at the camera again and shifted slightly, so that her ample bosom was well in focus.

'Cut,' shouted Phillip. 'Miss Parker now, please.'

David turned to watch as Claudia changed places with the other girl. She had a pantherlike grace all her own. Her voice was low and sexy as she read her lines. When she was finished, she casually shrugged her way back into her robe and went and sat down. Chocolate Box still bounced around the set.

'The Parker girl,' David said to Phillip. 'No contest.'

As he left the set, Claudia caught his eye. She smiled, and he felt a hint of promise in her smile. He returned to his office, packed up a few papers, called Linda to say he would be home for dinner, and then left.

Claudia was standing outside the building.

'Hello,' she said. 'Small world.'

They talked for a few minutes about the tests, and Beauty Maid soap, and the weather, and then David suggested dinner. Claudia said she thought that was a divine idea.

They went to an intimate Italian restaurant in
Chelsea, where David knew he was unlikely to be
spotted by any of his or Linda's friends. He called
Linda on the phone and made his excuses. She
sounded upset but understanding. Claudia called a
boyfriend and cancelled him out. They ate cannelloni
and talked and held hands, and there it all began.

Suddenly Claudia returned from the bathroom.
'Darling, what have you been doing?' she questioned.

David pulled her down on the bed. 'Thinking
about you, and how you picked me up.'

'It's not true!' she protested. 'You're just a dirty old
man who fancied me as soon as you saw me in that
bath!' She was wearing her white terry-cloth robe
again. David ran his hands underneath it. She
shivered. The phone rang. 'Saved by the bell,' she
giggled and rolled over to answer it. It was her agent.

David dressed slowly, watching her all the time.
She spoke animatedly on the phone, occasionally
pausing to stick out a small pink tongue at him. Finally
she hung up. 'Oh, you're dressed,' she said
accusingly. 'I've got simply marvellous news. I have
an interview with Conrad Lee tomorrow. He's over
here looking for a completely new face to star in his
latest film; it's all about the Virgin Mary or something.
Anyway, I'm to see him tomorrow night at six, in his
suite at the Plaza Carlton. Isn't that exciting?'

David wasn't pleased. 'Why do you have to see
him at night? What's wrong with during the day?'

'Baby, don't be so silly. My God, if he wants to get
laid, he can get it just as well in the morning as any
other time.' She marched crossly over to the dressing
table and meticulously started to apply her makeup.

'All right. I'm sorry I spoke. I just don't know why you want this stupid career of yours. Why don't you—'

'Why don't I what?' she interrupted coldly. 'Give it all up and marry you? And what do you suggest we do with your wife and kids, and all your other various family entanglements?'

He was silent.

'Look, baby.' Her voice softened. 'I don't bug you about things, so just forget it. You don't own me, and I don't own you, and that's the way it should be.' She applied lip gloss with a flourish. 'I'm starving. What about lunch?'

They went to their little Italian restaurant and good humour was restored.

'Sunday's such a dreary day,' said Claudia. 'It just sort of sags along.' She drank her red wine with relish and smiled at the short, fat proprietor, who grinned happily back. 'Do you know, everyone believes they are beautiful; I'm sure of it. They look in the mirror, and they see two eyes, a nose, and a mouth, and that's it, they think – what a gas!'

Her laughter lit up the restaurant, and David laughed with her. She was such a beautiful, vital girl. He had had affairs outside marriage before, but this was different; this time, for the first time, he wished he was free.

'I met this man once,' said Claudia. 'He promised me a yacht in the south of France, a villa in Cuba, lots of jewels and all that jazz, and then he just disappeared. I heard later he was a spy and got shot. Isn't life funny?'

After lunch they drove through the West End looking for a film they would like to see.

'Look at all those nuts,' exclaimed Claudia, watching a large procession heading toward Trafalgar Square. 'Can you imagine spending all your spare time rushing around tying yourself to embassies, and sitting down all over the place? And all the fellas have beards. I wonder why.' She snuggled up closer to David. 'Let's forget about the movie. Let's go back to my place and screw. I feel like getting laid again, don't you?'

Who was he to argue?

Chapter Two

BAN THE BOMB, the banner attached to the stout lady's back announced quite clearly.

PEACE EVERYWHERE, declared a large notice held aloft by a bearded young man.

END NUCLEAR WARFARE, stated a ragged piece of cardboard clutched gamely by a harassed woman, also clutching two scruffy-looking children by the hand.

This group, along with several hundred others, marched slowly into Trafalgar Square. Many had arrived before them, and there was a milling crowd around Nelson's Column and the fountains.

Linda Cooper was already there. She was squashed between an earnest-looking group of young girls with long, untidy hair and grubby-looking outfits, and a bespectacled gentleman who kept up a constant muttering to himself.

Linda was an attractive woman in her early thirties, with short auburn hair partly concealed beneath a chiffon scarf. She wore a cream Chanel suit which looked out of place in the company she was with. One would imagine that ten years earlier she had been very pretty indeed, but the prettiness had been replaced with an expression of resignation. There were little lines, a certain amount of tiredness, and slightly too much makeup, but the overall effect was attractive.

She glanced around. It seemed funny to be standing there, part of the crowd, without David. It was so seldom that she did anything or went anywhere without him, but more and more lately there had been long business trips and late meetings, and he seemed to have become so completely involved in his work, almost to the exclusion of all else. She sighed. It was only by chance really that she was at the meeting today. David was away, and suddenly she felt she must get out of the house and do something different for a change. The children were in the country with her parents for the weekend. She had declined to go, thinking that David would be home, but at the last moment he had had to rush off as usual. She had found herself alone, and eventually decided she couldn't bear to sit around the house all day, so she had phoned Monica and Jack and they had asked her over to lunch. But it was a mistake; they were really David's friends from his bachelor days, and she always sensed a certain forced gaiety about them, a sort of 'so David finally married you' attitude, 'well, he could have done worse.' After an hour and a half she excused herself on the pretext that she had to get home, there was so much to be done before the children arrived. What, she could not imagine, but Monica and Jack didn't argue, so she left.

It was while she was driving home that she noticed the marchers and the banners and the crowds, and on impulse she parked her Mini in a side street and made her way into Trafalgar Square, which appeared to be the general gathering point.

It was a subject she had often thought about and secretly wished that she could be part of. To protest seemed the very least one could do, if not for oneself, for one's children.

The end of an era was taking place. Nineteen sixty-nine and people were speaking out. She wanted to be one of them.

The bespectacled man standing beside her suddenly looked at his watch. 'It's three o'clock,' he announced excitedly.

There was a sudden surge forward of the crowd, and a general shouting and yelling. Small groups of people seemed to disintegrate from the mass and rush toward the road, where they promptly sat down in front of the traffic. Linda was carried forward with the crush and found herself near the edge of the pavement. There were a lot of policemen pushing and dragging and lifting the squatters from the road. As soon as one person was removed, another immediately took his place. The mob was delighted. They chanted various slogans and cheered and booed the police. The large blue police vans gradually began to fill up, but undaunted, new squatters appeared.

Linda felt marvellous. 'Ban the Bomb,' she shouted. *She* was protesting about the bomb. *She* was actually involved in a meeting of worldwide interest. *She* was, in a minute way, helping to protect the future of her children. It was an exciting experience.

'Ban the Bomb,' joined in the people near her.

'Come on, darlin'.' A dark-haired young man grabbed her by the arm, and together they rushed onto the road. They sat in the face of an oncoming taxi, and the irate taxi driver growled, 'Bloody barmy, the lot of 'em.'

Linda had a feeling of complete exhilaration, and then a pink-faced constable was grabbing her under the arms and pulling her to the side of the road. She started to struggle and another policeman joined them and took hold of her legs. There was a moment of immodesty as she felt her skirt hike up above her knees and then they unceremoniously dumped her back on the pavement.

Helping hands got her to her feet, where she discovered she had lost her shoes and somehow or other cut her arm. Her scarf had vanished and her hair fell around her face.

'You look a right mess, don't you?' It was the dark-haired young man again. 'Want to give it another try?'

A girl grabbed him by the arm. 'Oh, come on, Paul,' she said. 'Let's go. We don't want to get lumbered down to Bow Street again.' She was small, with long, pale-yellow hair, and she was very young.

Paul ignored her. 'Look,' he said to Linda, 'you had better come with us. I've got a mate lives near here and we can maybe get you some shoes.'

'Well…' started Linda.

'Let's not hang about, Paul,' said the girl crossly.

'All right,' decided Linda, and the three of them started to push their way to the edge of the crowd.

Paul took hold of her arm and guided her through the mass of people. His lank-haired girlfriend trailed miserably behind.

'My name's Paul Bedford. What's yours?'

Linda glanced at him. He was tall, with slate-grey eyes. She guessed he must be about twenty-two. She found him uncomfortably attractive.

'Mrs. Cooper,' she said firmly.

11

He gave her an odd look, half-amused, half-puzzled. 'Mrs. Cooper, huh?'

The pavement was cold and hard on her stockinged feet, and she found herself wishing she was safely home and not rushing around Trafalgar Square with some strange young man whom she had only met ten minutes before.

'I have a car parked close by,' she said. 'I think it would be better if I got back to it. I'm sure I have some old shoes in the trunk.'

But Paul was already leading her across the road into Newport Street. 'We're here,' he said, banging on a battered yellow door. 'At least come up. We'll bandage your arm, and then I'll take you back to your car.'

The girlfriend looked sulky.

'All right,' said Linda.

A makeupless, white-faced, black-haired girl finally came to the door. She wore a tattered blue-and-gold brocade Chinese housecoat and once-white fur slippers. 'Hi, baby,' she greeted Paul brightly. 'And how's little Mel?' She nodded at the girlfriend. 'Come on up.'

They followed her up a narrow staircase into an enormous room painted completely black. There was a large bed in one corner, a lot of books and cushions scattered around, and a record player with Miles Davis turned up full volume. This appeared to be the full extent of furnishings.

'Where's your old man?' asked Paul.

'He went down to join the crowd,' said the girl.

'We need a drink,' said Paul. 'Got hung up in the middle of it. This is Mrs. Cooper. She cut her arm and lost her shoes. Had a right punch-up.'

The girl smiled. 'You always manage to involve people. Sit down and I'll get you a beer. It's all we've got.'

'Come on,' said Paul to Linda, 'we'll fix your arm up.' He took her into the bathroom, which was surprisingly white and antiseptic-looking. 'So where's Mr. Cooper then?' he asked.

She looked at him coolly. 'He's away on business.'

'What's your name when it's not Mrs. Cooper?'

She hesitated, then said, 'Linda. Why?'

'I just wanted to know.'

They looked at each other for a long moment before she glanced nervously at the floor. This is ridiculous, she thought. What am I doing here with this boy? What would David think? I must get out.

They discovered a box of Band-aids and Paul put one over the cut on her arm. 'Was this your first meeting?'

'Yes,' she replied. 'Look, I simply must get back to my car now. It's really awfully nice of you to have taken all this trouble, but I have people expecting me at home, and they will be worried if I'm late.'

'Fine,' he said, 'I'll take you. Can't have you wandering about London with no shoes on.'

They went back into the large black room. Lank-haired Melanie was sitting clutching a can of beer. She jumped up when Paul came in and rushed over to him. Linda decided she wasn't very pretty, much too thin, and that awful hair!

'Have some beer,' Melanie offered. She had a whiny voice.

'No, we're splitting,' said Paul. 'I'll be back soon. You wait here.'

The girl obviously wanted to argue but didn't quite dare.

Paul kissed the owner of the room. 'I'll be back,' he said.

Linda said good-bye, and they left.

In the street he took her arm again, but she shook it free saying, 'I don't like my arm held.'

'What *do* you like?'

She didn't reply.

They walked in silence to where her car was parked. She felt embarrassed and inelegant in her stockinged feet. Besides, the pavement was cold and hard and she wished she was safely home.

When they reached her car he helped her in. 'Where do you live?' he inquired politely.

'Finchley. We have a house there.'

'Hey, we're neighbours. I live in Hampstead.' He stood on the pavement leaning against the car door. 'You can drop me there. Do you mind?'

'I thought you had to go back for your girlfriend,' she said nervously. She just wanted to drive off and leave him standing there. She knew how attracted she was to him, and somehow she felt very vulnerable.

'That's all right. Mel will find her own way home. She usually does anyway.' He walked around to the passenger seat and got in.

It's now or never, she thought. Either I tell him to get out or I'm accepting the fact that he's interested and letting him know that I'm interested too. She felt him staring. She started the car.

Linda drove expertly through the traffic. Paul sat silently beside her, his silence making her even more aware of his presence. Eventually she spoke. 'Your girlfriend isn't going to be too pleased with you, saying you would be back and then just disappearing.'

'It doesn't matter.'

They lapsed into silence again. She decided that when they reached Hampstead she would stop the car, wait for him to get out, and then wave good-bye and drive quickly away. She would give him no chance to talk about seeing her again. Instinctively she knew he would want to.

'I noticed you immediately,' he said.

'What?' she replied, startled.

'I said I noticed you immediately,' he repeated, 'in the crowd. You looked out of it, sort of lost. You wanted to be part of it and yet couldn't quite make it. So I grabbed your arm and pulled you into the road and then you were all right, you forgot yourself, y'know?'

'I don't know what you mean,' she said defensively.

'Oh, come off it, you know exactly what I mean.' He yawned rudely. 'Where's your old man then? Where's your kids? You *have* got kids, haven't you?'

'Yes. How do you know?' she said defensively.

'Easy. I can sum you up in a minute. Married maybe ten years, nice little house, husband away a lot, kids growing up and leaving you behind. It's true, isn't it?'

Her first reaction was one of anger, stop the car and tell this rude little boy to get out. But wait a moment, what he was saying was very near the truth. Wait, hear him out, what harm could it do? She was curious too. How did he know? Did she look the part so completely?

She forced a smile. 'You're very sure of yourself, aren't you?'

'Yes, I am. I can see it in your face. The way you look. Everything about you.'

'We've reached Hampstead,' she said quickly, and swerved the little car abruptly into the kerb. 'Thanks for the summing up. It was great fun for you, I'm sure. David would have been amused. Good-bye.' She stared straight ahead and waited for him to get out.

He didn't move, just said quietly, 'Can I see you again?'

She turned to look at him. His eyes penetrated deep into her own.

'I don't understand you. First you dissect my life, pull me to pieces, and then you ask to see me again. No, you can't. I'm in love with my husband. I have two wonderful children and I live a very nice life, thank you. I think you are pushy and rude. Please get out of my car and go away.'

'I would like to see you again. I think you need someone like me.' He opened the door and got out. 'Anyway, if you change your mind, I'm in the phone book.' He turned and walked away.

She watched him go. He's a creep, she thought angrily. He's very thin, probably never eats. So young, but so knowing. *I would like to sleep with him.*

She halted her train of thought abruptly. I would like to *what?* she asked herself incredulously. Sex had always been synonymous with David. She had never had an affair, she had gone to her marriage bed a virgin, and now this thought was in her head. Oh, there had been many boys she had dated, necked with, before getting married, but never anything more serious than that. David is a wonderful husband, she thought, a wonderful lover. But when did he ever make love to her these days? Maybe once a fortnight, and then it was a quick ten-minute affair out of which she derived no particular pleasure, and afterward he would turn over, go straight to sleep and snore, and she would lie awake for a long time thinking how it used to be before the children, when they were first married.

She sighed and started the car. It was impossible to turn the clock back.

* * *

The house was empty; even the dogs were away with the children, and their live-in Spanish maid, Ana, was out for the day. It was depressing. Linda switched the television on in the bedroom and noticed that it was nearly six. David had said he would be home around nine, so there were three hours to kill. She had no intention of watching television, but it was nice to have human voices around her. She decided to phone her mother and see how Jane and Stephen were behaving themselves.

Her mother's voice was placid and comfortable. 'Hello, Linda, dear.'

'Hello, Mother. How's everything?'

'Oh, fine, dear, fine. Jane's having her bath now and Stephen's right here. Wait a minute, hang on, he wants to speak to you.'

There was a pause, and then Stephen's thin excitable voice came on the line. He was eight. 'Hello, Mummy. We're having a smashing time. Grandma made lots of gooey cakes for tea, and that pig Jane tried to eat them all, so I pushed her off the chair and

17

she started to cry and…' He carried on at great length about the cakes, and then her mother's voice came back on the line.

'Daddy will be driving the children back after lunch tomorrow, so you should expect them around four. How is David? Did you have a nice peaceful weekend together?'

'Yes, Mother, very peaceful,' replied Linda ruefully. 'All right, then. I'll speak to you later in the week. Thanks for having the children. Kiss Janey for me. Bye.'

What now? Feeling slightly hungry, she went to the kitchen, but she hated cooking just for herself, so she finally settled for a cheese sandwich. There seemed nothing else left to do except to go to bed and wait for David.

Bed, David, the two thoughts connected in her head, and an idea formed. She rushed to her closet and hunted around until she found what she was looking for. A slinky black negligee she had bought in Paris several years ago and never really got around to wearing. It had always seemed too frivolous. She held it up against her and then returned to the kitchen to iron it. Well, this is what they say in all the women's magazines, she thought, smiling. Shock your husband into realizing how utterly sexy and devastating you really are!

After the negligee was ironed, she ran a long, hot bath and borrowed some of Janey's Baby Bubbles to throw in. For good measure she added some Chanel No. 5 cologne, until it all looked very luxurious and inviting. Next she creamed her face, set her hair, and then climbed into the bath and relaxed.

The phone rang. Wrapped in a bath towel, trailing bubbles, she hurried into the bedroom to answer it.

'Hello.'

'Hello, Linda?'

'Yes.'

'This is Paul Bedford.' A long silence, and then his voice again. 'You mentioned David and Finchley, so it was easy to trace you in the phone book. Look, I'm sorry, I wanted to apologize for earlier. I didn't mean to upset you. Will you forgive me?'

'There's nothing to forgive,' she said coolly. 'It certainly didn't bother me one way or the other.' She was tempted to say good-bye and hang up, but she waited to see what he would say next.

'That's all right then.' He sounded relieved. 'You know, when I like people, I mean really like them, I always seem to come on too strong. I don't intend to, but it just happens. Sort of reverse action.' He paused, then continued. 'A friend of mine is having a party tonight; he lives near you, and I thought you might like to come.'

'I'm sorry, I can't,' she answered quickly.

'No harm in trying. Maybe some other time.'

'You'll have to excuse me, I'm in the middle of taking a bath.' Then she added, 'Thanks for the thought, anyway. Good-bye, Paul.'

'Good-bye, Linda. Sorry about dragging you out of the bath. The party doesn't start until ten, so if you should decide you want to go, my number is Hampstead 09911. Bye.' He hung up.

0-double-nine-double-one. So easy to remember. She shivered and made her way quickly back to the bathroom. The bubbles in the bath had gone flat, and the water, when she got back in, was lukewarm. She was secretly pleased that Paul had phoned; it made her feel desirable and wanted, a feeling she couldn't remember having had for a long time. Tonight things would be different. She would make David realize that everything could and should be as romantic as it was when they first knew each other. After all, just because two people were married didn't mean that romance had to go by the board. I'm only thirty-three, she thought; that's still very young. Well, certainly not old. She climbed out of the bath and studied her body in the bathroom mirror. I could do with going on a diet, she mused. Her legs were shapely but a little heavy around the thighs, her waist was quite slim, and her breasts, although large and full, were still firm.

She slipped into the negligee. It clung flatteringly, and she was pleased with the effect. She applied a light makeup and combed out her hair. Then she turned off the television and put on the stereo. Sinatra was much more acceptable than some stupid sit-com.

The stage was set, the player was ready, it was nearly nine. A glass of wine would be nice, she thought. There was a bottle of rosé in the fridge, so she went and got it.

* * *

An hour passed. The wine was drunk, Sinatra was silent. The black negligee had been replaced with something a little warmer. The television was back on and Linda huddled morosely in front of it, watching an old movie.

She was a little loaded. The emptiness of the house seemed to press around her. Where was David? He had said nine o'clock. If he was going to be late, he could at least phone. Perhaps he had had a car accident. Perhaps he was lying badly injured or even…

The phone rang. First, the operator's cool efficient voice, and then David, obviously in a hurry. 'Look, I'm held up with these people here. I had to drive over from Leeds to Manchester, and I'm bushed. Not going to risk driving back tonight; it's a filthy night. I'll leave early in the morning and be home at eight.'

'But David, I'm expecting you.' She tried to keep her voice pleasant. 'Why couldn't you have let me know earlier? It's nearly ten, and you promised you'd be home by nine.'

'I can't talk now. I'll explain tomorrow.'

Her temper suddenly snapped. 'I don't care about tomorrow. What about *me?* I've had a bloody miserable weekend, and tonight I've just sat around waiting for you, and *you* couldn't even bother to phone. At least if I'd known I could have gone to the films or something. You're just selfish, and I can't—'

His voice was cold and unemotional. 'I'm with people now. I'll see you tomorrow. Good-bye.'

The line went dead. For a moment she sat very still trying to control a choking feeling of complete frustration. He had hung up on her, he hadn't even bothered to wait for her to say good-bye.

At last she replaced the receiver, only to pick it up again and dial. The ringing tone seemed very loud in her ear. I've had too much to drink, she thought vaguely. Then a voice was saying hello and she found herself replying with, 'Hello, Paul, this is Linda Cooper. About that party…'

Chapter Three

It was four o'clock when David and Claudia arrived back at her apartment. She lived in a converted house at the back of Knightsbridge, all very new and modern. She occupied the top apartment which had the advantage of a small roof garden.

David had often found himself wondering how she could afford it. All her furniture was new and obviously expensive, and she had an enormous wardrobe of clothes. She was an actress and model, and from what he knew of both professions, unless you were extremely successful you didn't earn a lot of money. Certainly not enough to keep Claudia in the style she obviously liked. He had mulled this problem over and come to no satisfactory conclusion. Eventually he had decided that she must have a rich father, although this didn't really tie in with the bits and pieces he knew of her background.

According to Claudia she had left home at fifteen, and arrived in London five years ago all set to be a movie star. Now she was twenty, very beautiful and sparkled like champagne. But no movie star.

He had known her only three weeks and in that time seen her as much as twelve times. She was always available, there didn't appear to be any other man in the picture. She accepted the fact that he was married, and didn't nag about it as a lot of women might. She never mentioned money to him. He had seen that she did the Beauty Maid commercial, but apart from that she hadn't worked at all.

He decided that he had to find out more about her. Maybe she needed money and was embarrassed to mention it. He resolved to bring the subject up.

When they entered, Claudia rushed about making a great show of fixing the bed and generally tidying up. She was most undomesticated. A cleaning woman came in every day except for weekends. She made a disgusted 'ugh' when she came to the dirty dishes in the kitchen.

David followed her in. 'I'll buy you a dishwashing machine,' he said, slipping his arms around her waist.

She turned, laughing. 'You're joking, of course. A dishwasher! What a *terrible* present. I'll have something more romantic than that, thank you!'

'What do you want? We'll go shopping tomorrow.'

'I want, let me see now. I want a Ferrari, two mink coats, lots of diamonds, a beautiful penthouse in New York, and a villa on the Riviera!' She started to laugh. 'Can you afford me?'

'I'm serious. Will you settle for a mink jacket? Go and order it tomorrow!'

She stared at him and licked her lips. 'I'd adore that. But if you want me to have it, surprise me. None of this ordering jazz. I like surprises.'

He grinned. 'A surprise it will be.' He wondered if now was the time to bring up her financial situation, and decided against it. Later, when they were in bed.

'When do you turn into Cinderella tonight?' she asked suddenly.

'I should leave about eight-thirty.' He stroked her hair. 'But I can always stretch a point, depending on what the main attraction is.'

She giggled and pulled off her sweater. 'The second feature is starting now. The main attraction should prove to be very interesting indeed!'

* * *

Sometime later, when David looked at his watch, he was surprised to find it was well after nine. Claudia lay asleep beside him, her long hair in disarray around her face, her makeup smudged and faded. She looked very young. Her clothes were scattered around the bedroom, leading in a trail from the kitchen. As if she sensed him looking at her, she opened her eyes, yawned, stretched, and made contented noises.

'You're like a cat,' he said, 'sometimes an innocent little kitten and sometimes the wildest, dirtiest alley cat around.'

'I like that. I can see myself telling it to someone in the years to come. There was this guy, and he said to me, you're like a cat, sometimes—'

He put his hand over her mouth. 'Don't say that. There will be no other guys, only me. I love you and I want to marry you.' He surprised himself with the words, but there they were, spoken aloud for all to hear.

'You know, it's amazing,' she said, 'how very simple it is for married men to propose. I guess it's an easy thing for them to say, because really they are all safe and secure, and they know they can lay out this tasty bit of bait without a hope in hell of getting trapped themselves. Marry me, my darling, only don't let my wife find out!'

He was furious. So, all right, he hadn't really meant it. Correction, he *had* meant it, but, as she had said, he was secure in the knowledge that it was not

24

possible. However, the fact that she realized this infuriated him. Why did women always seem to have so much insight into the things men said?

'I could get a divorce,' he offered.

'Are you going to?' she replied coolly.

'I don't know.' He pulled her to him. 'It's not just me and Linda; there's the children to consider. But I do love you, and one day, when my kids are a little bit older, well then, everything will be okay. In the meantime I can look after you. I don't want you to work. No more interviews. I'll give you money.'

She stared up at him with her large, slanty green eyes. 'I'm glad you have it all figured out.' She caressed his back and he felt desire rise up in him again. She had only to touch him and he wanted her. 'There's only one little problem. I don't want to marry you. Not even if you were free, and we could rush off and do it now.' She wriggled away from him and got off the bed. She stood looking at him, completely naked, and continued, 'I want to do what I want to do, whenever I want. No ties, no strings. I don't want marriage, it means nothing to me. So don't offer it like it's a golden hoop, because I'm just not going to jump. So I love you now, today. But tomorrow, who knows? That's me. I don't pretend to be someone I'm not, so why don't you do the same?'

He couldn't control the choking excitement he felt. Her words didn't matter. He dragged her back on the bed and let loose his fury and frustrations. She tried to struggle but he crushed her beneath him until her struggling stopped and became part of him.

For David it was devastating; when he was with Claudia it always was. Each time it was more, emotionally *and* physically.

'You'd better get up. It's past the witching hour, and wifey will be waiting.' She stretched languidly.

'Don't be a bitch. Anyway, I think I'll stay.'

She kissed him. They phoned Linda, and Claudia pretended to be the operator so that the call appeared to be long distance.

Afterward she said, 'No bastard would talk to me that way and get away with it. I feel sorry for your wife.'

'Do you?' he said shortly. It annoyed him when she discussed Linda.

'Yes, I do, although it's her own fault.'

'What do you mean by that?'

'What made me more exciting to you than her? Because I'm newer and younger and prettier. Am I prettier?'

'Yes, you're prettier.'

'But you shouldn't *have* to look around. She should make bloody sure that she's always new to you. Most women seem to get married and then stop trying. We've caught the fish, now we can put away the bait and only bring it out on special occasions. I'm not saying that you wouldn't screw around once in a while. All men do, even the happiest of married men. But that's all it would be. There would be no affairs like me; you wouldn't need them.'

'Thank you, Marriage Counsellor Parker, but I have a feeling that you are addressing the wrong party.'

'Shall I speak to your wife? What shall I say? "Darling, in strict confidence, I'm banging your husband. This isn't really necessary. If only you weren't so dullsville he might fancy you again. Liven up a bit, and back he will come."'

They both started to laugh. 'You *are* a bitch. Is that why I love you?'

'No,' she giggled. 'You *know* why you love me.'

They got up and she busied herself in the kitchen making sandwiches while David prowled around the flat thinking how he could bring up the subject of her finances again. She had annoyed him with her little speech about not wanting to marry. But really he wasn't too annoyed, because on thinking it over he decided she had only said it as a defence mechanism. She knew they couldn't get married, so to save face she had probably convinced herself that she didn't want marriage anyway. On thinking it over even further, he was almost pleased, because it put him in the enviable position of being able to have his cake and eat it too. He didn't really want to leave Linda. In his own way he loved her, although she had ceased to attract him sexually shortly after they were married. He had compensated for this by different affairs throughout the years, and to Linda he had been more than generous materially. She was the perfect wife figure. A lovely hostess and mother.

No, he certainly didn't want to leave Linda. He felt no particular guilt about being unfaithful to her. Although if *she* was to him… But no, that was unthinkable. The very idea of Linda being unfaithful was ridiculous.

Claudia was licking mayonnaise off her fingers in the kitchen. She wore a pink kimono and had tied her hair away from her face.

'You look about fifteen,' he said.

'And you look about fifty. What *is* on your mind? Are you brooding because I turned down your gallant proposal?'

'I want to talk to you seriously. Bring the sandwiches and come and sit down.'

She followed him into the living room, and munching a sandwich, sat down on the floor near his feet. 'What seems to be bothering you, David?'

'Look, darling. I've been thinking a lot about you.'

She laughed. 'I should hope so.'

'This is serious,' he continued. 'I've been worried about how you manage financially. This apartment can't be cheap, and I want to help you out. I mean, frankly, where *do* you get your money?'

She sat very still. Her eyes glinted dangerously. However, she managed to keep her voice pleasant. 'Well, baby,' she said sweetly, 'what makes you want to know?'

He didn't observe the danger signals. 'Of course I want to know. Do you get an allowance from your father, or what?'

'Come *on*. I haven't seen my family in five years, and I don't care if I ever see them again. My old man wouldn't give me a penny to go to the bathroom with.' She sat silently then, and David realized that she had no intention of answering him.

'Claudia, I want to know,' he said sharply.

She arose. 'I don't like being questioned. I'm not asking you for anything. I don't want *anything* from you!' She started to shout. 'Leave me alone with your questions. What's on your mind? Where do you think I get my money from? Do you think I'm a whore? Well, if I was, wouldn't I be asking you for money?' She was crying now, and he was shocked that he had provoked such anger. 'It's *my* business where I get my money from, and if you don't like the idea of that, then let's just forget it,' she yelled.

He caught her mood of fury. 'All right,' he said coldly, 'we'll forget it.' He marched into the bedroom and dressed. She didn't follow him.

When he came out, she was sitting on the sofa reading a magazine and didn't look up.

He stood there, undecided about whether to walk out or not. 'Are you going to tell me?' he demanded.

She continued reading and didn't answer him.

'Good-bye,' he said, and left.

In the hall outside her front door he immediately regretted this move. He couldn't go home, and he debated making it up with Claudia, but that was impossible. If he gave way to her now, he would be admitting defeat, and he never admitted defeat to any woman. No, he decided, let her burn a little, and she would soon come running back. They always did.

He went downstairs to his car, having decided to spend the night in a Turkish bath. He was puzzled about why Claudia was so secretive about the source of her income; it could only mean that there was something he wouldn't like. Well, in that case, when she told him, he would stop it, whatever it was, and then she would be dependent on him, which was exactly the way he wanted it.

He drove to the Turkish baths in Jermyn Street, and after going through the hot and cold steam baths and having a massage, he was quite happy to settle down in his small white cubicle, where he promptly fell asleep. Tomorrow he would settle everything.

Chapter Four

Paul looked younger than Linda remembered him. He was wearing a black sweater and tight black trousers. She had decided to wear a plain dark-blue dress after discarding several other outfits. They met at a prearranged spot. Paul helped her out of her car and said he would drive, as he knew the way.

'I'm glad you changed your mind. What did it? My unbelievable charm?' He grinned.

'I don't know.' All the wine she had drunk and the rushing to get ready had finally made her tired. 'Maybe I shouldn't have come. I don't know why I'm here, really.'

He looked at her. 'I'm glad you're here. I don't think you'll be sorry you came. In fact, I promise you that.'

They drove a short way along the Heath until Paul pulled into the drive of an old rambling house. Its windows were ablaze with lights, and the belting voice of Solomon Burke screamed out from the stereo. A couple were arguing in the open doorway, and, as they arrived, several more people came pushing through the door with much laughter and yelling. Paul parked the car and they went in.

The scene that greeted their eyes was wild to say the least. The front door led into a small hall with big rooms off either side of it and a large staircase in the centre. The staircase was littered with various people, a lot of men with beards, girls sitting and standing, and everyone steadily drinking. The room on the right was filled with couples, dancing or just standing and necking. There appeared to be no furniture, only a rather battered stereo set balanced precariously on the windowsill. The room on the left featured a thin girl with stringy red hair taking off her clothes to the beat of some bongos being hammered on by a West Indian clad only in white shorts. No one was taking much notice of them. Mostly people were watching a blond boy at the other end of the room, who was standing on a chair, quite naked, reciting an obscene poem.

Paul squeezed Linda's arm. 'Come on,' he said, leading her up the stairs, greeting people as he went. 'Let's get rid of your coat. Then we can get a drink.'

Upstairs there were more rooms equally devoid of furniture. Paul steered her into a room with a bed creaking under the weight of many coats. Two girls were staring deep into each other's eyes in a corner, and another girl was either asleep or had passed out at the bottom of the bed.

Linda took off her coat and felt too dressed up in her neat blue dress. Paul said that she looked great, and took her to find a drink. They went downstairs to the room on the left. The redhead had abandoned her strip and was sitting on the floor, someone's sweater covering her. She grabbed hold of Paul's leg as he went by. 'Hello, sexy. Wanna make it?' Her voice was slurred. 'I've got a great body. How 'bout you?'

Linda found herself separated from Paul, so she headed toward a table where the drinks appeared to be coming from.

A fat man pounced up behind her. 'You look very smart,' he said. 'Who *are* you?' His face was beaded with sweat and his breath a combination of onions and stale beer. 'You want a drink?'

'Yes, please,' she said, trying to edge away from the full blast of his breath.

He poured her a very large Scotch in a cracked glass. She drank it down hastily.

'Let us go and dance,' he said, and put his arm around her waist. She could feel the hotness of his hand penetrate her dress through to her skin.

'Not just now,' she said, trying to disentangle herself.

He licked his pudgy lips, and then Paul arrived. 'Hello, Bruno. I see you've met Linda.'

The fat man removed his arm. 'Oh, she's yours, is she?' he said hastily. 'I don't know what they see in you.' He wiped his mouth with a plump pink hand and ambled away.

Paul laughed. 'Don't take any notice of him,' he said, and then was suddenly serious. 'You're great, you know that?' He took her hand.

'Thank you,' she said. She had never been able to accept compliments easily. Quickly she drained her glass. 'I'd like another drink.'

He poured her a large Scotch which she drank down fast, feeling its burning effect almost immediately. 'I think I should go home,' she said weakly. 'I'm almost drunk, you know.'

'I know.' He pushed her toward the wall, and then leaned forward and kissed her.

She closed her eyes as she felt the intimacy of his tongue penetrate her lips. His mouth was persistent and demanding. She felt she should push him away but didn't have the strength, and anyway, she didn't want to. It was a long time since she had been kissed like this. David never kissed her anymore, and she had forgotten how exciting it could be.

'Oh, so here you are.' The whiny voice was familiar, the note of anger unmistakable. Paul straightened up. Melanie was standing there, her yellow hair hanging in a straight curtain around her thin, flushed face. 'I thought you were coming back for me.' She glared at Linda. 'Or have you been so busy that you couldn't find time?'

'I'm sorry, Mel, thought I said I'd see you here.'

'Well, you didn't.' Her voice was becoming shrill. 'And how's Mrs. Cooper? Recovered, I see.'

'Can it, Mel,' said Paul abruptly. He steered her away from Linda and into the hall. 'Look, I'm sorry, but that's the way it is.'

'That's the way what is?' Her dull eyes filled with tears.

'It's been great, but we've been heading this way a long time now, and it's best to forget it. I still like you and all that bit, but, well, you know…'

'No, I don't know. And anyway, what can you see in that old bag in there?' She started to cry. 'I hate you, Paul.'

'Look, kid, you're seventeen, there'll be lots of other guys. You'll soon forget me. We're just not—'

'We're not what?' she interrupted angrily. 'God, I hate you!'

He shrugged and walked away. Linda was deep in conversation with the fat man again. 'Do you want to go?' he asked.

'No.' Her eyes were bright. She was now very drunk. 'Bruno's going to teach me a new dance.'

'Bruno can find a girlfriend of his own. I'll teach you anything you want to know.' He warned Bruno off with a look, took her into the other room where the dancing was going on, and held her very tight. 'I want to sleep with you,' he whispered.

'I want to sleep with you too,' she whispered back. 'I mean, I don't want to, but it would be nice, but I… Oh, God, I think I had better get some air.'

He kissed her again. This time she kissed him back, and their mouths met in mutual enjoyment. They stood still among the dancers, lost in their own little world. His tongue explored her mouth, and she felt a sudden urgent desire for him. He pressed her very close and then released her.

'You wait here,' he said. 'I'll get your coat.'

She stood patiently waiting, the liquor she had drunk falling over her in waves. She couldn't think clearly at all, her head buzzed, and she wanted to be back again in the safety of Paul's arms. There was a lot of noise coming from the hall, and she wandered out there. Two men were fighting. It was the fat man, Bruno, and the West Indian who had been playing the bongos earlier. They screamed obscenities at each other and rolled about on the floor. No one tried to stop them.

'Why are they fighting?' she asked a girl standing near her.

'Oh, darling, Bruno always has to fight with someone,' the girl said. 'It wouldn't be Bruno if he didn't.'

The West Indian's nose began to bleed, and there was a lot of blood. Linda suddenly felt sick. She edged her way to the front door and out. The cold air had a slightly sobering effect. She went over to her car and sat in it.

Eventually Paul arrived. 'I was worried. I thought you'd walked out on me.' He got in the car and put his arm around her. She pulled away. 'What's the matter?' he continued.

'I feel terrible. I think I'm going to be sick.'

'Oh, great. Let's go back inside and I'll get you upstairs to the bathroom.'

'No. I don't want to go back in there.'

'You'll feel better in a minute.' He put his arm around her again, and this time she didn't pull away. He kissed her, while his hands explored her body.

She felt weak and her head spun, and when she shut her eyes everything whirled round and round. She could feel Paul touching her, and his mouth on hers, but it all seemed like it was happening to someone else.

Abruptly he let go of her and started the car. They seemed to be driving for ages, but really it was no time at all. Then he was helping her out of the car, and they were climbing a lot of stairs, and then they were in a room, and he was pushing her onto a bed.

She didn't struggle when he unzipped her dress and pulled it off, because, after all, this wasn't really happening.

He kissed her slowly. The bed was soft, and she felt very comfortable. His arms were strong and warm, and his hands created a fantastic excitement in her. He rolled her over on her stomach and she felt him undoing her bra.

'I'm not here,' she whispered. 'I'm on another planet. I'm very drunk, you shouldn't take disadvantage of me. I'm at an advantage...' She started to giggle.

He began to kiss her back, and then she was suddenly lost in a raging passion which seemed to go on forever and ever.

'I love you,' one of them said.

'I love you,' the other said.

It was good to be wanted.

* * *

Linda awoke at five in the morning. She opened her eyes in disbelief, and was parched with an awful thirst. Her eyes felt heavy and her face like sandpaper. She looked around and discovered she was in a small untidy room. Paul was sprawled across the end of the bed asleep.

She sat up slowly and looked for something to cover herself with. Her head felt it would split open if she moved too rapidly. She pulled a cover off the bed, and wrapping it round her, she got up.

Paul didn't stir. She groped her way to the door and found herself in a tiny hallway piled high with clutter. She made her way through to the bathroom, which was small, rusting, and old. She switched on the light. It was a naked bulb, and when she turned on the cold-water tap a large black spider ran disdainfully across the basin. She almost screamed.

Quickly she drank four mugfuls of water. It tasted faintly of toothpaste but made her feel a little better in spite of that.

She stared in the mirror above the basin. Her makeup was smeared and etched into deep lines about her face. Her hair was untidy and matted. I look like I belong here, she thought vaguely.

She padded back into the bedroom and searched for her clothes. When she found them she dressed quickly. She looked at Paul. He slept deeply. She stared at him for a long time and then, finding her coat, she left.

It was cold and silent in the street. Her car coughed and spluttered, and she thought that it would never start. At last it did, and she drove home through the deserted streets.

She let herself quietly into the house and went straight to her bedroom. Everything looked clean and new. She took a hot bath and then collapsed into bed, where she lay and thought. She felt tremendously guilty, and angry at herself for having allowed it to happen. Yes, she had been drunk, but was that any real excuse? She had never imagined herself in the role of the unfaithful wife and it was not something she accepted easily.

What would David say?

Why was her first thought always of David?

At last she fell asleep knowing that in the morning she would have to face him, and that wasn't going to be easy.

She tossed and turned. It was a long and restless sleep.

Chapter Five

David left the Turkish baths at eight in the morning feeling refreshed and invigorated. He contemplated phoning Claudia but then decided to wait the day out and see if *she* called *him*.

He parked his car, bought the morning papers, and then made his way along Park Lane to the Grosvenor House Hotel where he planned to breakfast before going home.

He ordered bacon, eggs, toast, and coffee, and sat back to scan the papers. His eye was immediately caught by a half-page picture on the front page of the *Daily Mirror.* It was captioned MORE NEAR-RIOTS IN TRAFALGAR SQUARE, and the picture was of an angry mob of people surrounding two policemen who were in the process of carrying a woman away from the road. The woman's skirt was high above her knees, so high that you could glimpse her panties. Her hair was flopping over her face, and one shoe was about to fall from her struggling foot. It was an effective picture.

The waitress arrived with his breakfast order. She was plump and cockney. She peered over his shoulder at the paper. ''Ere, what does she think she looks like?' she muttered. 'About time all this rubbish was stopped. A load of showoffs, that's what they are. They should lock the lot of 'em up!' She wandered away, cluck-clucking about nothing in particular. David stared at the photo, horrified. The woman was unmistakably Linda. His Linda! He shook his head in disbelief. What was she doing? What was she thinking of?

He gulped his coffee, scalded his tongue, swore, found himself unable to eat anything, and called for the check.

The waitress padded slowly back. 'What's the matter, dear? Everything all right?'

He thrust money at her. 'Everything's fine,' he said and stormed out.

A parking warden was in attendance beside his car. David brushed impatiently past him.

'I'm afraid you'll have to wait while I finish writing out this ticket, sir,' said the warden. 'I suppose you are aware that this is a restricted zone for parking?'

'Just give me the ticket and get on with it,' said David brusquely.

The warden glared at him and then proceeded to take his time.

David drove away, his face grim. He envisaged what he would say to Linda. The whole thing was so utterly ridiculous. His wife at a protest meeting! It was ludicrous. She didn't know anything about politics or bombs. The kitchen, the children, and social activities such as tea with the girls and dinner out twice a week were her province. Ban the Bomb indeed! Who did she think she was?

Claudia was forgotten. He put his foot hard down on the accelerator and raced home.

Ana let him in. 'Mrs. Cooper, she sleep late,' she announced. 'You like tea?'

'No,' he grunted, already halfway up the stairs to the bedroom.

Linda was asleep, curled up and buried beneath the covers. He drew the curtains, throwing glaring daylight into the room. She didn't stir. He paced the floor, coughed loudly, and when she still didn't appear to show any signs of waking, he went over and shook her roughly, thrusting a copy of the *Daily Mirror* in front of her face as she sleepily opened her eyes.

'What's all this about?' he demanded angrily.

Oh, God, he had found out about her and Paul! How? So soon. She sat up quickly.

David stood there glowering at her as he continued talking. 'What is this? Some secret ambition to make yourself look a complete fool?' He brandished the paper at her again, and she took it from him.

A feeling of relief swept over her when she realized that this was what he was so furious about. 'What an awful photo!' she exclaimed. 'I didn't know they were taking pictures.'

'Is that all you have to say?' He mimicked her. 'I didn't know they were taking pictures!' He snatched the paper away and in a loud and angry voice said, 'What were you doing there anyway? What were you thinking of?'

'I had nothing else to do. I just found myself there. I'm sorry that you're so angry about it.'

'I'm not angry,' he screamed. 'I like to see photos of my wife smeared all over the papers, with her skirt around her waist, accompanied by a load of layabouts.'

She got out of bed. 'I'm not going to sit here while you yell at me. Perhaps if you spent a weekend at home for a change this might not have happened.'

Just then the telephone rang. Linda suddenly felt very hot and flushed. Supposing it was Paul? Should she answer it, or would it be best to let David pick it up, and then maybe Paul would hang up. She was convinced it was him.

David swooped down on it and barked into the receiver, 'Yes?'

Linda held her breath, while David launched into a long conversation with someone from his office. She took advantage of his preoccupation on the phone and dressed.

When he had finished talking, he seemed a little calmer.

'Do you want some breakfast?' she asked.

'No. I have to make some calls. There's this party tonight to launch the Beauty Maid soap product; I had forgotten all about it. You had better meet me at the office at seven, and we'll go from there. I hope to Christ nobody saw your publicity.'

She groaned inwardly at the thought of another party, and then mentally planned her day, which included being at home to greet the children and a visit to the hairdresser's.

David meanwhile had his own thoughts. Claudia would most certainly be at the party, she was being paid to be there. He wondered if it would be possible for him to effect a quiet reconciliation without everyone in the room noticing. Had to be sure that Linda didn't become suspicious, she seemed to be getting a little too concerned about him being away so much. Maybe she was beginning to suspect him, although this seemed unlikely, as he had managed to get away with various affairs throughout the years and she had never found him out yet. At least he would be able to see Claudia. He started to make his business calls.

* * *

The children burst back into the house at exactly four o'clock. Linda's father was always prompt. She had just returned from the hairdresser's, and Stephen flung his small, wiry body at her, practically knocking her down.

'We've had a smashing time, Mummy,' he exclaimed. 'I'm starving. What's for tea? Grandma makes lovely cakes!'

His sister, Jane, gave Linda a small kiss. She was six and rather shy. 'I'm glad we're home, Mummy. Your hair looks all pretty. Are you and Daddy going out?'

Linda greeted her father and they sat and chatted while Ana served tea and the children rushed around rediscovering their various toys.

She was only half listening as her father droned on about Stephen's and Jane's activities during the weekend. She thought about Paul. What did he think of her? Why *hadn't* he telephoned? What would she say if he phoned and David was there?

Finally her father left, and when the children were settled with Ana, having their dinner, she began to get ready. Just as she was about to leave the house, the telephone rang. She so expected it to be Paul that she felt herself break out in a sweat and her hand started to shake as she picked up the receiver. 'Hello.'

'Hello, darling, it's Monica. How about *you*, then! Aren't *you* the dark horse! Fancy leaving us yesterday and not saying a word about where you were going. What does David think about it all?'

'Oh,' replied Linda, 'he's not too pleased.'

Monica laughed. 'Not to worry. Jack and I think it's marvellous. Anyway, sweetie, we're having a few people over after dinner tonight, and we would *love* you and David to come.'

'I don't know, Monica. We have to go to a press party launching the new soap product. I can't say what time we'll be able to get away.'

'Never mind. Just come along when you're finished. You know us, we're *always* late.' She gave no chance to protest. 'See you later, then. Bye.'

Linda replaced the receiver. She really wasn't too fond of Monica and Jack, and certainly didn't feel like seeing them later. However, she would have to tell David, and he would probably want to go.

She left the house in a bad mood, with a headache, half-angry and half-relieved that Paul hadn't phoned. She desperately wanted him to, otherwise, what had it all been? A quick one-night affair? A meeting of two people with no more in common than a few hours in bed? However, if he *did* phone, she wanted to tell him that she couldn't possibly see him again, that it had all been a big mistake.

She sighed. At least that way she would be regaining a small amount of self-respect by denying herself something she really wanted. It was all so unexpected. She had really never thought of herself as the sort of woman who could have an affair. And Paul was so much younger than she, and so different from the type of people she knew and mixed with. How had it happened?

She searched her mind and finally concluded that it must be her fault. She resolved to try and put the episode out of her mind and to work desperately to make things more satisfactory between herself and David.

That decision made, she felt better.

* * *

It was nine o'clock before Claudia appeared at the Beauty Maid party. David had been watching for her all evening, and suddenly there she was. She materialized beside him, looking exceptionally beautiful, and murmured, 'Good evening, Mr. Cooper.'

He was taken off guard. He was standing talking to a group which included several press and Linda. He became flustered.

Claudia noticed and smiled faintly. People were looking expectantly at him, waiting to be introduced. At last he said, 'Oh, this is Claudia Parker, our Beauty Maid girl.'

Claudia smiled at the group. She was flushed and her eyes shone. David knew at once that she was a little drunk. She wore an orange dress, dangerously low cut, and the women in the gathering found themselves standing up straighter and throwing out their bosoms, as if in answer to this sudden challenge. The men were all obviously impressed.

'Miss Parker?' Ned Rice, a small beady-eyed reporter, pressed toward her. 'What do you *really* think of Beauty Maid soap?' His eyes darted toward her bosom.

Claudia played up to him. She fluttered her very long eyelashes and gave him one of her deep, sexy looks. 'Well,' she said at last, 'actually, I'm an actress, therefore I don't feel I can give you a serious opinion on soap. As a matter of fact, I've just come from seeing Conrad Lee, and he's very interested in having me in his new movie.' She shot David a triumphant look.

Ned Rice was most interested. 'Sounds wonderful. Perhaps we could do a piece about you on our film page.'

'Yes, I'd like that.' She smiled. 'I'll give you my phone number.'

David could stand it no more. He gripped her by the arm, smiled tightly, and said, 'I hope you will excuse us. Miss Parker is here for a purpose. She will be demonstrating our product, and I think she's due to begin pretty soon, so I had better get her over to Phillip Abbottson.'

'Oh, well, Miss Parker,' said Ned Rice, 'I'll see you later and we'll get together on this.'

'Fine.' She gave one last radiant smile around the group and followed David.

As soon as they were out of earshot he exploded. 'You're drunk,' he accused. 'Where have you been? You were supposed to be here by eight.'

She gave him a cool look. 'David, baby, you're nothing in my life, so why don't you just leave me alone?'

'You fucking bitch,' he said in a low voice. His grip tightened on her arm.

'I'm going to make a scene if you don't let go of me,' she said quietly. 'I'm tired of you telling me what I should do. I'm not someone's wife who has to answer questions and account for *every* second of her life.'

At that moment Phillip Abbottson rushed up to them.

'What *is* going on?' he asked. 'Claudia, you were supposed to be here an hour ago. We're waiting to unveil the display. Get changed, for Christ's sake. You think we want to be here all night?' He gave David an odd look and then with Claudia in tow rushed off again.

Ned Rice sidled up to David. His plump, pasty wife was talking to Linda across the other side of the room. 'Quite a bit, your Miss Parker,' he said with a leer. 'I bet she's a hot little number, a real tiger.'

David endeavoured to remain calm. 'I wouldn't know.'

'In that case I expect it's all right for me to have a bash.' He nudged David. 'These starlets are all the same, y'know. You've just got to tell them you can get their name in print and they open their legs without you even asking.'

David was saved from answering by the arrival of Mrs. Rice and Linda from across the room.

Ned affectionately patted his wife's plump shoulder. 'Enjoying yourself, love?' he asked. Then he waggled an accusing finger at Linda. 'And what were you up to, making front-page news this morning?'

David was beginning to dislike Ned Rice more and more.

Just then the lights in the room were dimmed and a spotlight was focused on a mock stage set at one end of the room. Phillip Abbottson was standing poised at a microphone. As soon as the chatter died down he launched into a long speech about Beauty Maid soap. He was a good promoter and made a simple bar of soap sound like a solid block of gold. At the end of his speech there was polite scattered applause, and then he stood to one side and said, 'And now I would like to introduce you to Miss Beauty Maid herself!'

The curtains were drawn back, and there sat Claudia, in a marble bath surrounded by bubbles, in fact, an exact replica of the set that was used in the television commercial. She was wearing a flesh-coloured swimsuit, but of course no one could see it, so the general assumption was that she had nothing on beneath the bubbles.

David felt a surge of excitement.

Claudia smiled at her audience and started to recite her Beauty Maid speech.

Ned Rice whispered something obscene in David's ear.

Mrs. Rice said to Linda, 'Isn't she a pretty little thing?'

Linda stared blankly into space, her thoughts on the night before.

When Claudia finished speaking there was hearty applause from the men and a few jealous titters from the women. Then the curtains were drawn and Phillip appeared back at the microphone with more to say.

David excused himself and made his way behind the stage. The marble bath was now empty, and he noticed a small door at the back of the dais. He hesitated and then went through it.

Claudia was patting herself dry with a towel. She was in a very small office and her clothes were scattered around in her usual untidy style. She was wearing the flesh-coloured swimsuit, which clung to her like a second skin.

She looked at him wearily. 'What now?'

He walked over to her and put his hands on her shoulders. 'I'm sorry,' he said. 'No more questions.'

She threw him her wide-eyed look. 'Promise?'

'I promise.'

She smiled and snaked her arms around his neck. 'All right, you're forgiven.'

He bent down and kissed her warm, soft lips. Her body was still wet as he put his hands in the top of her swimsuit and slowly peeled it down.

'Not here, you idiot,' she whispered. 'Someone might come in. Anyway, you'll be missed.'

He let go of her and went and turned the key in the lock.

She was giggling softly. 'Oh, David, you really like to take chances.'

He cupped her breasts in his hands and bent to kiss them. She moaned, 'Go on then, you son of a bitch. Do whatever you want, I don't give a damn!'

Chapter Six

The gathering at Monica and Jack's was in full swing when Linda and David arrived. It was a mixed crowd, for Monica liked 'group variety', as she put it. Monica herself was a largish woman heading rapidly toward forty and desperately trying to pull back the other way. She had a lot of very-bright-red hair, which was inclined to be frizzy, and her face, although heavily laden with Elizabeth Arden, was somewhat outdoorsy and even a little horsey. She used a heavy, overpowering, musky perfume which enveloped you like her personality, and was given to talking in a shrieky sort of a voice, her conversation always well peppered with 'dahling' and 'sweetie' and 'oh, my God!'

Jack, in contrast, was rather reserved. He was a little older than David, but they had been close friends for a number of years. He smoked a pipe and had a twirly grey moustache. He always wore suede jerkins or some sort of similar sporty attire. One could imagine him with an enormous mansion tucked away in some rural part of England, walking a large dog through his spacious grounds. He owned a chain of garages and in his younger days had fancied himself as a racing driver. Even now he would often take a test spin on the track to keep his hand in.

Monica grabbed Linda when she arrived, and proudly, with her arm around her, she marched her into the living room and announced dramatically, 'And this is our famous ban the bomber!'

Linda was terribly embarrassed. Monica made her sound like some new type of aeroplane! She knew most of the people there, and they all made some sign of greeting. There was one couple she hadn't met before, a thickset, very dark man, and a silver-blond, haughty-looking girl. Monica, as soon as she had finished with her dramatic announcement, introduced her.

'I'd like you to meet Jay and Lori Grossman, friends of mine from America. Jay's here to direct the new Conrad Lee picture.'

'Really,' said Linda. 'How interesting. I met a girl earlier this evening who's going to be in it.'

Jay raised a quizzical eyebrow.
'That *is* interesting.' He spoke with a short, sharp, New York accent. 'We haven't cast at all yet, apart from the male star.'

Linda smiled. 'I expect she's suffering from delusions.'

'What's her name, anyway?' Jay asked.

Linda frowned. 'I can't really remember. My husband will know. She just did a commercial for his company.'

Just then Monica arrived with David and made the introductions again. He had been in a very good mood since leaving the other party. He put his arm around Linda and started to chat easily to the Grossmans.

'Darling,' Linda interrupted him, 'what was the name of that little girl who was doing the Beauty Maid thing?'

'What?' he asked, feeling immediately guilty. 'Why do you want to know?'

Linda looked at him strangely, or anyway he thought she did. 'Do I have to have a reason?' she asked.

He felt the tension build in the short silence that followed, and then he laughed weakly and said, 'Of course not. It's Claudia Parker. Why?'

Jay shook his head. 'Never heard of her.'

'What is this?' questioned David.

'Well,' said Linda, 'you remember she said she was going to be in the new Conrad Lee picture. Jay's directing it. I thought he would know about her. Anyway, apparently she isn't in it or going to be.'

'She didn't say she was in it at all,' said David coldly. 'She said she had been to see Conrad Lee and he liked her, that's all.'

Jay laughed. 'That accounts for the confusion. Conrad is always seeing these poor little broads and stringing them along. Confidentially, the girl is already cast. An unknown Italian kid of sixteen. It builds up the publicity for the film. If we put on a big search for the right girl and Conrad enjoys seeing them, it makes everyone happy.'

David scowled at him. 'Everyone is happy except the girls whose hopes he builds up.'

Jay shrugged. 'That's show biz. Most of them know the score, and the ones that don't soon learn.' He turned to his wife, who so far hadn't opened her mouth. 'Isn't that so, sweetheart?'

Lori Grossman nodded. Her face never seemed to register any expression. It was like that of a beautiful, but quite blank, painted doll.

'That's how Lori and I met,' Jay continued. 'She was an actress, came for a part, and instead got me. She's my third wife. The other two were actresses as well. I probably met them the same way. Don't even remember now.'

At last Lori spoke. Her voice was a thick Southern drawl. 'I sure would like another drink, honey.'

'Certainly, baby.' Jay stood up. 'How about you, Mrs. Cooper?'

'Please call me Linda. I'd love a gin and tonic.'

Jay went off to fetch the drinks, and Monica arrived back and claimed Linda, dragging her over to some other people to show them the famous newspaper clipping.

Lori crossed long shapely legs.

David's eyes wandered. 'What part of America are you from?' he asked pleasantly.

'I come from Georgia, honey.' She blinked lazily at him. 'But I've lived in Hollywood for the last five years.'

He studied her. She was older than Claudia, about twenty-seven, he reckoned. She looked like one of those thin models out of *Vogue*magazine, everything carefully perfect. He found himself attracted to her. The very perfection made him wonder what she was like in bed. He wondered if that beautiful chignon of silver-blond hair stayed in place; one somehow couldn't imagine her with it out of place. 'How long are you here for?' he asked.

'Several months, I guess,' she drawled. She apparently had no conversation except to answer questions.

There was a silence until David said, 'You and your husband must come over to our house for dinner one night.'

'That would be fun.' She smiled, displaying two rows of even, white, obviously capped teeth.

Jay returned with the drinks. 'Where's that lovely wife of yours?' he asked.

'Honey, there's no ice in this drink,' said Lori petulantly.

'Screw the ice,' said Jay. 'This is England, baby, they don't go so big on the ice bit.' He turned to David. 'Listen, we have to meet some friends soon at the Candy Club. How about you and Linda coming along with us?'

'This is our second party tonight, and I don't know how tired Linda is, but it sounds like a good idea to me,' David said. 'I'll ask her.'

'Hell, you must come,' said Jay. 'Lori does the craziest dancing you've ever seen. I'll go ask Linda myself.' He went off.

Lori said, 'Gee, honey, what do you do without ice!'

David laughed. 'We usually have ice. We're not that uncivilized. I suppose they've run out.'

She screwed up her nose. 'I like ice,' she stated, and then stared blankly off into space.

He looked at his watch. It was past twelve. Claudia would be safely in bed. She had promised that she was going straight home. 'You've left me fit for nothing else!' she had joked. He wondered if he could telephone her, but then decided it was too late. He didn't want to wake her, and anyway there was nowhere really private that he could phone from. The

Candy Club sounded like a good idea, and Lori Grossman's dancing even better.

Jay returned with Linda, smiling broadly. 'I never get no for an answer,' he said with a wink. 'We're all set. Shall we make a move?'

Monica was quite frosty when she found David and Linda departing with the Grossmans. 'Honestly, darlings,' she complained, 'you've only been here two seconds!'

However, they left, and piled into David's Jaguar.

Lori was wrapped in a full-length black-diamond mink coat. It reminded David that he had promised Claudia a jacket. He would get it the next day, she had been so sweet earlier. Or was sweet the right word?

Linda and Jay hit it off very well. They chatted about the differences between England and America, and schools, and where it was best to bring up children. It seemed Jay had three children, all from his previous marriages. Eventually he said to David, 'Hey, your wife is beautiful *and* intelligent, quite a combination.'

Linda was beginning to feel much better, her headache had gone, and she had had just enough to drink to take away any tiredness. She pushed Paul to the back of her mind and was enjoying talking to Jay.

They arrived at the nightclub. Jay asked to be taken straight to Conrad Lee's table.

The great Conrad Lee was a tall, voluble, half-French, half-White Russian man in his late fifties. He was totally bald, very suntanned, with piercing eyes which seemed to glare right through you, even in the dimness of the nightclub.

He was at a table with six other people, and he leaped up and embraced Lori. When Linda was introduced he kissed her hand. He smelled strongly of garlic.

The waiters busied themselves trying to squeeze more chairs around the already crowded table while Jay attempted introductions, but it was more or less hopeless as the noise of the band was so loud that you couldn't hear yourself speak.

David stared in amazement and fury at Claudia. She sat beside Conrad, her hair tousled, one strap of her dress falling off her shoulder revealing much cleavage. She was very drunk. When Conrad sat down his hand caressed her shoulder, pushing the other strap of her dress down. There was another girl on the other side of Conrad, a plump brunette. He had his arm around her too, pinching chunks of her fleshy back between his fingers.

'Got two lovely little girls here,' Conrad said to Jay, and then with a wink, 'Maybe we can use them in the picture.'

Jay raised an eyebrow at Linda. 'See what I mean?' he said with a smile.

'That's the girl I was talking about,' Linda whispered.

'Sure,' said Jay. 'She's got as much chance of getting in the picture as a fly!'

Claudia noticed David then. She was too drunk to be surprised or shocked. She just waved gaily and said, 'What a small world!'

David remembered her saying those exact words to him the first time they met. He scowled at her.

Conrad took Lori off to dance, then Jay claimed Linda, and they went off to dance too.

David sat down in the empty chair beside Claudia.

'You lousy bitch!' he said in a low voice. 'Going straight home to bed – well, I suppose you'll be doing that eventually.'

She looked surprised. 'Baby, what's the matter? I *did* go home, and then Conrad called and said he would like to see me again, so he could come to some decision about the part. I have to think about my career, don't I?'

'You're drunk,' he said in disgust. 'You're acting like a cheap whore. Do you honestly believe all this shit Conrad is feeding you about putting you in his stinking film? I credited you with more brains than that.'

She looked at him coldly. 'Shut up. You make me sick. You're just jealous, that's all. The only time you act sweet is when you've got a hard-on!'

He wanted to slap her. She sat there, glaring at him, and for one lucid moment he saw not his beautiful Claudia, but a hard calculating face over a well-developed, highly exhibited body.

'Your tits are hanging out!' he said.

'So?' she replied. 'Why not? Are you the only one that's supposed to see them?'

The plump brunette the other side of David suddenly tugged his arm. 'Are you a film producer too?' she asked. Her eyes were large and round and somewhat bloodshot.

'No,' he said curtly.

Conrad and Lori returned to the table. David stood up. Lori was very tall. She stood there remote and cool. David could see that Claudia was watching her jealously. He took hold of Lori's arm quickly.

'What about another dance?' he said. 'I want to see this wild dancing of yours.'

Claudia shot him a dirty look and then focused her charm on Conrad again.

'That would be fun, honey,' drawled Lori, and they headed for the dance floor.

She danced beautifully. 'I used to be a showgirl in Vegas,' she confided.

The evening dragged on. Claudia got drunker and drunker, and she and Conrad closer and closer. The plump brunette was obviously forgotten. Linda and Jay chatted on. Lori sat silently, only speaking when someone spoke to her. David lounged morosely, watching Claudia and Conrad and occasionally attempting to flirt with Lori in case Claudia might be watching *him.*

At two in the morning Linda said with a yawn, 'I think we had better be going. I'm absolutely exhausted.'

No one else in the party seemed interested in leaving, so they said their good-byes. Claudia said good-bye with a drunken smile and then turned to concentrate on Conrad, who by this time was as drunk as she was.

Jay insisted on coming with them to the car where they exchanged phone numbers and promised to all get together again soon.

At last they were alone. Linda leaned back in the car and closed her eyes.

David said, not really meaning it, but wanting to take his bad temper out on someone, 'You and that phony director were getting very friendly.'

She opened her eyes. 'No more friendly than you and that trampy soap model.'

He shot her a dark look. 'I didn't even talk to her. I don't know what you mean.'

'Oh, David, really,' she sighed. 'You didn't even talk to *anyone,*you were so annoyed she was with Conrad Lee. Any fool could see that.' She paused, then added curiously, 'Have you ever taken her out?'

He stared furiously at the road ahead. 'What a ridiculous question.'

'I just wondered. You seemed so interested in her. Even at the first party you kept on getting in little huddles with her.'

'She works for us, Linda. I was trying to see that the display thing went off smoothly, that's all.'

They lapsed into silence. He switched the car radio on.

'Darling,' Linda said quickly, tentatively, 'what's wrong?'

'What do you mean, what's wrong?'

'I mean, what's wrong with us? What's happening to us? Why are we so far apart all of a sudden?'

He turned off the radio. 'I didn't know we were so far apart.'

She looked out of the car window – they were driving through the park, and the trees looked dark and ominous as they sped past them. 'It's funny, David, this must have been starting to happen to us for years, and yet neither of us realized it, neither of us tried to stop it. We're almost like strangers now, and the only thing we have in common is the children.'

'I think you're overtired, you're talking a lot of nonsense.'

'A lot of nonsense,' she repeated. 'Is that what you really think?' Tears started to roll silently down her cheeks. 'When did you last make love to me? When did you last *want* to?'

'Oh, so that's what this is about.'

She fought to keep her tears under control. 'No, that's not what this is about, but it's part of it.'

He pulled the car onto the side of the road and stopped.

Then he turned to face her. What could he say? That he didn't find her exciting anymore? That Claudia was a better lay? She was right, really, they were far apart.

'Do you remember our honeymoon?' she questioned.

Yes, he remembered their honeymoon. Spain, hot and sticky, and long pleasurable nights with Linda, an innocent young Linda, who awoke all sorts of desires and ambitions in him. 'Yes, I remember our honeymoon,' he said quietly.

'Why can't things be like they were then?' She looked at him plaintively.

'Linda, we're both ten years older. Things don't stand still, you know.'

'Yes, I know.' She thought – Paul makes me feel ten years younger. He makes me feel attractive and desirable. He makes me feel wanted.

David said, 'We'd better be getting home. I need to get to the office early in the morning.'

'Yes, all right.' She thought, why don't you take me in your arms? Why don't you throw me down on the back seat and make love to me here? Why don't you worry about what *I* need?

They drove home in an uneasy silence, both realizing that there was more unsaid than said.

The house seemed cold and dark. Linda went in to look at the children. Jane slept curled up in a ball, her thumb stuck firmly in her mouth. Stephen had kicked all his covers off and nearly fallen out of bed. She covered him and kissed him lightly on the forehead. They were so innocent, her two precious children. So young and pure.

David was taking a shower. Linda undressed and settled into bed. She wondered if because of what she had said he would want to make love tonight.

He didn't. He returned from the bathroom, got into bed, switched the light off, muttered, 'Good night,' and appeared to go straight off to sleep.

She lay there angry and frustrated. I tried, she thought. I really tried to talk to him. But he doesn't seem to care what's happening to us, he doesn't seem to *mind.*

* * *

The morning dawned bleak and raining.

David was up at seven. He shaved, showered, and dressed without disturbing Linda. He was out of the house by eight.

She awoke shortly after. Jane was standing beside the bed. 'Mummy, can I come in for a cuddle, please?' the little girl requested.

'Yes, of course, darling.'

'I hate Stevie,' Jane confided. 'He's a nasty, rough boy. I wish boys were girls!'

'Yes, that's a very good idea,' replied Linda, smiling.

The morning passed in a flurry of domesticity. The children started school the following day and there was a lot to be done. School uniforms to be assembled, books to be found, everything washed and clean.

Linda had no time to think, and in the afternoon she had promised to take them to a movie.

There was no message from Paul. She was both hurt and yet relieved.

When they returned from the cinema she phoned David. He wasn't in the office so she left a message for him to call her as soon as he returned. Jay Grossman had phoned and left a number. She rang him back.

'We were wondering if you and David would care to join us for dinner tomorrow night?' he said. 'Lori just can't wait to go to the Savoy Grill – she's heard Princess Margaret goes there and figures we're bound to be at the next table!'

Linda laughed. 'I'll have to check with David. Can you call back later?'

David didn't phone until past seven. 'I'll be late,' he said shortly.

'How late?'

'I don't know, probably around twelve.'

'Where do you have to go?'

His voice was angry. 'What is this, a cross-examination?'

She replied coldly, 'No, it's not a cross-examination, but I think I'm entitled to know why you're going to be late.'

There was a silence, then, 'I'm sorry, of course you are. I'm tired, I suppose. Actually, I've got a late meeting with Phillip.'

'Why don't you bring him back here and I'll give you both dinner?'

'No, it's all right. We'll grab a sandwich next door and get on with things.'

'I'll see you later, then.'

'Yes, don't wait up.' He hesitated, then asked, 'How are the children?'

'They're fine. In a state of excitement about school tomorrow.'

'Give them a kiss for me. Bye.'

'Bye.' She hung up and yawned. It's an early night for me, she thought, then she remembered that Jay would be phoning back about dinner the following evening. Quickly she picked up the phone and dialled David's private number at the office. It rang and rang, but there was no reply.

She hung up and went and looked in the phone book for Phillip's number. David was probably in *his* office. She couldn't find Phillip's number, but his home number was there, so she dialled that. His wife, Mary, answered.

'I'm sorry to bother you,' said Linda, 'but can you give me Phillip's private number at the office?'

'Yes, of course,' said Mary, sounding slightly surprised. 'I'm expecting him home any minute, so I don't think there will be any reply.'

Now it was Linda's turn to sound surprised. 'But isn't he working late with David?'

'No, he's definitely on his way home. We've got his mother for dinner. He'll be here any minute.'

'Oh,' said Linda quietly, 'I must have made a mistake.'

'Hang on a sec,' said Mary. 'I think I hear him at the door now.'

Linda was left hanging numbly onto the receiver. She felt stunned. So David was lying. Why was he lying? How long had he been lying? And why was it only now, when she herself had been unfaithful, that she had to find out? It was obviously another woman. She felt sick.

Phillip's harsh voice boomed down the phone. 'Hello, Linda. What's your problem?'

She forced her voice to be light. 'No problem, Phillip, I'm just trying to track David down. I thought he said he was working with you, but I must have got it wrong.'

Phillip sounded embarrassed. 'I can't help you. David left the office early today.' He added as an afterthought, 'He's probably out with Mr. Smythson or someone from up north. We seem to have a whole group of people visiting this week.'

'Thank you, Phillip,' said Linda. She wanted to say, 'You don't have to try and make excuses for him.' Instead she said, 'I'm sure you're right. Good-bye.'

So this was the answer to her questions. It all tied in. Late nights home, weekends away on business, no real physical interest in her. This must have been subconsciously why she found herself in bed with Paul. They say there is a certain point in every marriage where a woman is at the crossroads as to whether to go to bed with someone else or not, and depending on the state of her marriage at the time, she makes her decision.

It's true, thought Linda, if things had been all right with David and me, then I would never have looked twice at Paul.

It all seemed so wrong, and to add insult to injury, Paul hadn't even rung her. She felt used. By both of them. And she didn't even know what move to make

next. Tears seemed threateningly and uselessly
close.

Chapter Seven

David awoke on Tuesday morning early, with one thought uppermost in his mind, and that was to get out of the house, reach a telephone, and phone Claudia.

It was seven o'clock, and Linda lay sleeping quietly, so quietly in fact that for a moment he contemplated using the phone in the house, but realizing the probable folly of this, decided against it.

He shaved, showered, dressed hurriedly, and left. He drove as far as Baker Street before stopping at a pay phone. He dialled the number and listened to it ring, but no one answered, so he redialled, but still no reply. He let it ring for a long time, but to no avail. At last he reached the obvious conclusion that she was either out or too deeply asleep to be disturbed.

He jumped back into his car, and with a sudden flash of decision drove to where she lived.

This time it was the doorbell he rang to no avail.

'Bitch!' he muttered to himself. 'Dirty little bitch!'

He hung around outside for a while, but eventually realizing the futility of this, he drove sourly to his office.

Every half-hour he rang her number, getting more and more angry each time it wasn't answered. At eleven it was finally picked up by her cleaning woman.

'Miss Parker,' he snapped.

The daily's voice was full of cockney richness. 'I fink she's asleep. 'Old on a tick. I'll go 'ave a look.' She returned after a short pause. 'She ain't in,' she stated. 'Any message?'

He said, 'You don't happen to know what time she went out?'

'Can't say that I do. Don't fink she's bin 'ere since yesterday, 'cos 'er bed ain't bin slept in.'

'Thank you,' he said. 'There's no message.'

He imagined her with Conrad. Her smooth, beautiful body crushed to his, going through the motions of love-making which she practised so expertly. He could almost hear her small exquisite cries of excitement, her little moans, and the way she muttered crude words in a low, throaty voice. He swore.

After that he rang her apartment every hour, putting the phone down when the cleaning woman answered. He was furious with himself for being so hung up about her. He had always prided himself on never getting too deeply involved emotionally, always being able to shut other people out of his life when he had had enough of them. But this time it was different. Whatever she did, he couldn't seem to get Claudia out of his mind.

At four o'clock she finally picked up her phone. The record player was very loud in the background, and she sounded in good spirits. He listened to her voice saying 'Hello,' then a pause, then – 'Hello, is anyone there?' Then another longer pause, and then – 'Oh, screw you, whoever it is!' And the phone was slammed down.

He left the office at once and drove straight over to where she lived. He didn't want to fight with her on the phone, he wanted to see her, hear the excuses, watch her lie.

She answered her front door and looked surprised and a little guilty to see him. She was wearing very tight white slacks and a mansized black sweater. Her face was devoid of any makeup, and although she looked tired, her brilliant green eyes shone with an alert, triumphant expression.

'Surprise, surprise!' she said. 'Come on in.'

He followed her into the flat. A very loud Rolling Stones 'Satisfaction' was turned up full volume. A half-bottle of Scotch and a giant pink fluffy toy poodle stood on the table.

'Want a drink?' she asked.

'It's four o'clock in the afternoon,' he said coldly.

'Oh, dear!' she muttered, like a naughty child caught doing something wrong. She poured herself a stiff Scotch, lit a cigarette, and flopped down on the floor. 'Well, David, what is there to say?'

'There's plenty to say.' He paced the room angrily and added menacingly, 'Plenty.'

She giggled. 'Do stop it with the wronged-husband bit. I *told* you I wasn't tied to anyone. I warned you that no man tells me what to do.'

He shook his head at her. 'I don't understand you. Sometimes you act like a cheap whore.'

She rolled over on her stomach, taking a long drag of her cigarette, and blowing the smoke toward him. Then she said calmly, 'I'm in a very good mood today, nothing can spoil it, not even you.'

She rolled onto her back and stretched, the taut outline of her breasts appearing through her sweater. He felt the familiar hot desire creep up on him.

'Conrad Lee is a very important man, and he's going to do a lot for me.'

'Sure, he'll do a lot for you,' said David bitterly. 'He'll do a lot for you in bed.'

'I'm testing this week for his new film. How about that?'

'Balls!'

'You're just jealous, that's all. You'll see, he's going to make a star out of me.'

'You're making a fool of yourself. The *director* of the film said that this is Conrad's hobby, stringing along little girls like you.'

'Come on, David dear. The last thing I am is a little girl. I'm nobody's fool. I know the score. *You* should know that.'

'How was he in the sack?'

Her eyes met his. They were big and green and bright. 'He wasn't anything like you.' She stood up and wrapped her arms around him. 'No one's like you,' she whispered. 'No one's ever been like you.' The fight was over.

It was slow, and warm, and tender. Afterward they lay on the floor where he had taken her, locked in each other's arms.

She kissed him softly. 'You must understand,' she whispered, 'it doesn't mean I don't love you. When I sleep with him, it's nothing. He's a pig, an old pig. But, baby, I want to be in his movie. I want to be in it *so much*. And I'm going to, I promise you that.'

He flicked his hands over her soft breasts. 'You're so beautiful, when I'm with you I don't care what you've been doing. So get in his lousy movie if you must. But don't sleep with him or anyone else again, or I'll beat the shit out of you!'

She pressed closer to him. 'I love it when you play tough.'

It's impossible, he thought, impossible that it can happen again so soon, and be that much better. She's like a tigress. They should cage her naked in the zoo for all to see, for only seeing is believing. And they should pin a notice to her cage – 'Do not feed. Only eats men.'

Out of the blue Claudia said, 'Your wife's very attractive, isn't she?'

'She used to be. I suppose she still is, really.'

'How old is she?' asked Claudia, a typical woman's question.

He wasn't interested in discussing Linda. 'Thirty something. I don't know.'

'I wonder what *I'll* look like when I'm thirty.'

He was saved from answering by the phone.

Claudia reluctantly lifted the receiver.

'Oh, hello,' she said softly. She glanced quickly over at David. He immediately wondered who it was. 'I'd like that,' she was saying. 'About what time?' She balanced the receiver under her chin and fumbled for a cigarette from the table. 'All right, see you tomorrow. Look forward to it.' She hung up. 'I'm starving!' she exclaimed. 'I feel like going out for a fabulous exciting dinner.'

'Who was that?' he asked, trying to keep his voice casual.

'Who was what?' she asked, knowing perfectly well what he meant.

'On the phone.'

She hesitated for just a second too long before saying, 'It was my agent. He wants me to have dinner with him and his wife tomorrow night.'

'Friendly of him, just like that he starts asking you to dinner.'

'Yes, just like that,' she said patiently. 'As a matter of fact, I called him earlier and told him I wanted to see him about this Conrad thing. I'm going to take a long bath. Can we go out later? Or have you got to rush home?'

He thought she was lying, but what was the point in arguing? 'Do you *want* me to be free?'

'Of course I do, otherwise I wouldn't have asked you.'

'I'll phone home. Where do you want to go? I'll book a table.'

'Let's go somewhere great for a change. We always have to hide out in some old dive. What does it matter if we're seen? After all, I *am*Miss Beauty Maid, so I'm business, really. Let's go to Carlo's.'

Carlo's was a very expensive, very fashionable Italian restaurant. It was *the* place to go, *the* place to be seen. David knew he was taking a ridiculous risk going there with Claudia. He was sure to see people he knew. However, on the other hand, he *wanted* to be seen with Claudia. He *wanted* people to know that she was his.

'OK, you go and make yourself pretty, and I'll book a table for eight o'clock.'

She kissed him lightly. 'Divine, darling.'

He gave her a playful tap on the bottom. 'Put some clothes on, or we'll never get out!'

Giggling, she retired to the bathroom.

He read the evening papers, booked a table at the restaurant. He felt guilty about phoning Linda, but eventually he did, and then snapped at her when she asked what he had to do. He produced some suitable

70

lies, felt badly about the whole thing, inquired after the children in a fit of conscience, and then hung up.

Claudia reappeared after a time, transformed. Her glossy ash-blond hair was piled on top of her head in studied confusion, her makeup was smooth and perfect. She wore a slinky black dress and rows and rows of jet beads. She looked stunning.

David told her so, and she smiled and preened and showed off her dress to him, flitting around the room like some beautiful exotic bird. 'Isn't it *exciting* going out somewhere *decent* together!' she exclaimed. 'I do wish we could do it more often.'

In the car on the way to the restaurant he had second thoughts. It was a stupid thing to do. Linda was bound to find out, and then what? Especially as she seemed to be so sensitive about their marriage lately. He glanced quickly over at Claudia. She was fiddling with the radio, trying to find music.

'Why don't we drive out somewhere nice in the country instead?'

She stared at him, her big eyes frosty. 'I knew you'd get cold feet. *You* go to the country. Let me out. I'm sick of hiding all over the place.'

'All right, we'll go to Carlo's.' To hell with it. Linda probably wouldn't find out. They said wives were always the last to know.

The restaurant was very crowded. The headwaiter said their table would be a few minutes, so they sat at the bar. Claudia greeted several people. David was relieved to see no one he knew.

A girl came up to them, dragging a weedy-looking young man behind her. She was thin and suntanned, and quite pretty. 'Gorgeous!' she said to Claudia. 'You look fabulous! Where *have* you been, haven't seen you for ages!' She dragged the young man alongside her. '*You*remember Jeremy.'

Jeremy blushed and stuttered, 'Hello.'

'We're engaged! Can you imagine!' She giggled and gave Jeremy a playful poke in the ribs. He looked acutely embarrassed.

'Shirley!' exclaimed Claudia. 'How marvellous!' She turned to David. 'Shirl, darling, this is David Cooper, a very old friend of mine.'

Shirley extended a small suntanned hand, and David shook it briefly.

Claudia continued, 'And, David, I'd like you to meet Shirley's fiancé, the Honourable Jeremy Francis.'

Jeremy edged forward. 'Jolly glad to meet you, old boy.' He had sandy-coloured skin, liberally dotted with angry red acne.

'Sit down and have a drink,' said Claudia. 'We must celebrate!'

They found extra chairs and sat down. The girls immediately went into a huddle about the dresses they were wearing. The Honourable Jeremy sat uncomfortably on the edge of his chair. He was extremely tall, and his knees bumped David's under the table.

'We're going to have an *enormous* wedding,' Shirley was now saying. 'It will be simply marvellous. Jeremy's parents know absolutely everyone!' She flashed a large emerald-and-diamond ring at Claudia. 'Look!' she said dramatically. 'Asprey's!'

Claudia said, 'It's divine. I love it. I'm so happy for you both.'

'And now, what about *you?*' questioned Shirley, shooting a meaningful look at David.

Claudia laughed. 'You know how *I* feel about marriage. It's not for me, Shirl baby. *I* like being single. Anyway, *you* met Jeremy first!'

Jeremy blushed and looked suitably flattered.

David stood up. 'I think our table's ready.'

'Did you *book?*' said Shirley wistfully. 'We forgot, and now we've got to wait simply ages for a table, and I'm *starving.* She hesitated for a second or two and then continued, 'I say, why don't we all have dinner together? I haven't seen you in *such* ages, Claudia, and it would be great fun!'

'We have a table for two,' said David grimly.

'We don't mind being a bit cramped, do we, Jeremy?'

Jeremy nodded blankly.

'What do you say?' Shirley turned to Claudia.

Claudia looked hopelessly at David. 'Fine, we'd love it.'

They followed the waiter to their table, Shirley waving and smiling to several people on the way.

'I think this is a simply marvellous place,' she said to Claudia as they reached their table. 'I'm sure if one sat here for a week one would see absolutely everyone one ever knew pass by, sort of like London airport!' She giggled loudly.

David sat through the dinner in sullen silence, and Jeremy didn't have much to say, so it was Shirley who did all the talking, with Claudia occasionally joining in. Shirley was an avid reader of *Queen* magazine, especially the society pages, and her main topics of conversation were who had been seen with whom, and what good parties were going on. Jeremy apparently was asked to most of them, and Shirley went into minute details about the most boring items.

For example, Lady Clarissa Colt wearing the same dress to two different parties, and the Honourable Amanda Lawrence having a coming-out party where they ran out of champagne. 'It was too awful,' wailed Shirley. 'One just *never* should run short of champers! Too embarrassing!'

Eventually, when they reached dessert, Jeremy took her off to the small dance floor where they clung limply together.

'Let's get out of here,' said David. 'I've heard just as much as I can take from the stupid, snotty cow.'

'I'm sorry, baby,' replied Claudia soothingly. 'She is a bit much.'

'A bit much? That's an understatement if ever I heard one. Who is she, anyway?'

A smile played softly around Claudia's mouth. 'When I first came to London, I worked in a club. Miss Fancy Pants worked there too.'

'What were you doing in a club?' asked David, surprised.

'I had to earn some money, and this actor I arrived with never seemed to work, so I took a job in a club.'

'Doing what?'

'The dance of the seven veils!' she laughed.

'What! You must be joking.'

Her smile faded slightly. 'I'm not joking. Look, I had no talent for doing anything else. It was either that or being a hostess and getting pawed about by a lot of dirty old men. I would sooner take my clothes off any day. They could look, but they couldn't touch.'

'I don't know anything about you, really, do I?'

Her large eyes turned suddenly remote. 'You've never bothered to listen. Like all men, your prime concern is to get me in the sack as fast as possible.'

There was a short silence, then she gave a quick, brittle laugh. 'I'm sorry, my past is a big drag anyway. Why *would* you want to hear about it?'

David was about to reply when Shirley and Jeremy returned.

'Jeremy's made the most divine suggestion,' said Shirley. 'There is a simply dinky little nightclub opened down at Windsor, and he says why don't we all pop down there.'

David looked at her sourly. 'At the Castle, naturally.'

For a moment Shirley's pale blue eyes glinted angrily, then she grimaced and laughed quickly, replying, 'No, sweetie, *not* at the Castle.'

'Count us out, then,' snapped David.

'I say, old chap, are you sure?' stammered Jeremy.

Claudia broke hurriedly into the conversation. 'David's tired. You two run along, and if we change our minds we'll join you later.'

'All right,' said Shirley, 'but *do* try and make it.' She grabbed Jeremy by the arm. 'Come along, sweetie, we'll leave these two lovebirds on their own.'

She shot a dark glance at David, waved gaily at Claudia, and towing Jeremy along behind her, they made their exit.

Claudia started to laugh.

'I don't happen to think it's so funny,' said David grimly. 'I suppose I'm stuck with the check as well. Many thanks for a delightful evening.'

Her laughter increased. 'I'm sorry. But honestly, it *is* funny. If you had known Shirley a few years ago – well, I mean, you just wouldn't believe it. She was anybody's and everybody's!'

His tone was cold. 'And you?'

Abruptly she stopped laughing. She stared at him for a few seconds and then said slowly and deliberately, 'I think we have just about reached the end of our relationship, if you could ever call it that.' Before he had a chance to reply, she got up from the table, and threading her way through the restaurant, vanished out of sight. Quickly he called for the check.

'It's David Cooper, isn't it?' The voice was loud and American.

David looked startled. There stood Jay Grossman. 'Well, hello,' he said uneasily.

'Where's Linda?' Jay stared pointedly at the recently occupied place across the table.

David wondered if he had seen Claudia leave, then decided he hadn't. Otherwise, as he was only a casual acquaintance, he would never have made such an obvious remark. 'She's at home,' said David, then indicating the rest of the table he continued, 'I had a business meeting and they all had to rush off.'

At that moment the waiter presented the check.

David threw down some money and quickly got up.

'Nice seeing you, Jay.'

Jay was not to be dismissed. 'Come and say hello to Lori. She'd be most upset if I told her I'd seen you and hadn't brought you over for a drink.'

'Only for a minute,' said David reluctantly. 'Linda's expecting me home.'

The Grossmans were sitting at a table across the other side of the room. David was pleased to note that they couldn't see his table from where they sat. Jay had only spotted him by chance on his way back from the men's room.

Lori looked as aloof and perfectly groomed as before, every shining blond strand of hair arranged carefully in place, her face a mask of flawless makeup. She wore a pale-brown chiffon dress, which dipped revealingly between her breasts.

'Nice to see you again,' said David, unable to keep his eyes from straying down her neckline.

'Likewise,' she replied in her faintly suggestive, empty drawl.

'Come on – sit down and have a drink,' said Jay.

'Well—' He sought wildly for an excuse, couldn't find one, and anyway, what the hell – eyes fixed firmly on Lori's neckline, he sat down.

'What'll you have?' asked Jay.

'A Scotch on the rocks.'

Jay summoned the waiter while Lori produced a small gold compact and proceeded to touch up an already perfect makeup.

'I spoke to Linda earlier,' Jay said. 'She mentioned she was going to talk to you about joining us for dinner tomorrow night.'

'Oh,' said David blankly. His mind was half on the fact that Claudia had walked out on him – what a bitch! – and half on the fact that he had a strong fancy for Mrs. Cool, Dumb Grossman. What a revelation to get her into bed and penetrate beneath the layers of makeup, eyelashes, and hair pieces. 'Good idea. Where do you want to go?'

'Lori rather likes the idea of the Savoy Grill.'

'Yeah.' Lori put down her compact for one brief moment. 'I've heard it's fantastic. You get to see Princess Margaret and that cute guy she's married to.'

'They don't exactly do a cabaret there,' said David, smiling. 'But they have been known to go there.'

Jay said, 'Shall we meet at our hotel?'

They chatted a short while longer, and then David made his excuses and left. He tipped the attendant who brought his car round and sat morosely in it. Screw little Miss Hot Pants Parker. She was becoming too much. First of all she talked him into going to a restaurant he didn't even want to go to. Then she lumbered him with her dreary friends. Then she admitted to working in a strip joint, and got insulted when he commented on it. And then she had the utter nerve to walk out on him!

On top of all this, she had been to bed with that fat slob of a producer the previous evening. She was nothing but a slut, an easy lay. If he wasn't careful he might even *catch* something from her.

She could get lost. He was going home.

He headed his car toward Hampstead. It was ten o'clock.

Chapter Eight

After a while Linda stopped crying. Where was *that* going to get her? She went into the bathroom and washed her face, then stared at her reflection in the mirror. She didn't know what to do. She knew she couldn't face the prospect of sitting around waiting for David to finally arrive home, fresh from the arms of some tramp. She had no one to telephone. Since marrying, she had gradually lost touch with all her girlfriends – they had all drifted apart, got married, and gone off to live in different parts of the country. She thought of phoning her mother, but to confide in her would be ridiculous. Her mother had never really approved of David and would be only too pleased. In desperation she phoned Monica.

Monica was cool. 'Absolutely charming the way you stayed five minutes and then dragged off my most important guests. I mean, really, darling – a bit off.'

Their conversation was brief, and when Linda hung up, she thought, the hell with it, I'm not a child, and she picked up the phone again and dialled Paul's number.

He answered immediately. 'Hello.'

She got cold feet and froze, not saying anything. Then she hung up in a panic.

He phoned back at once. 'Linda, this is Paul. I know you just called me.'

She was taken aback.

'Look – I've been *waiting* for you to phone. I knew you would. Can I see you? Can you come over?'

'When?' she muttered weakly.

'How about now?'

'I don't know…'

'Please, I must talk to you.'

'Well, all right. I'll be there in half an hour.'

'Great.' He gave her the address in case she had forgotten it.

She was surprised. Ego had told her that he would remember her, but she hadn't expected him to be *waiting* to see her, *expecting* her to phone.

She got ready swiftly before she changed her mind, and drove the five-minute distance to where he lived.

It was an old house converted into apartments, squashed between a butcher's shop and a vet on the main High Street. She climbed five flights of stairs before reaching number 8.

He answered her knock immediately.

'I don't really know what I'm doing here,' she blurted.

He took her by the hand and led her inside. 'You look lovely. I've been going mad waiting for you to phone.'

'Why didn't *you* phone me?'

'Look, Linda – I understand your scene. I don't want to put you in a bad position. It was up to you to make the next move.'

He made her feel very young, although she could give him at least ten years. 'I know nothing about you,' she murmured.

'You're always saying that,' he replied. He was wearing paint-stained faded Levis and a white sweater. He looked very attractive.

They were standing in a small, dark room with black walls hung with lots of paintings, some framed, some unframed, mostly nudes, with exotic thin faces, masses of hair, and voluptuous bodies. The only furniture was a teak Danish dining table – piled high with papers – and a battered old scarlet couch. She sat on the couch, and he offered her beer or vodka. She elected to have vodka.

He fixed her drink, then put a Billie Holliday record on and sat beside her.

'About the other night,' she began nervously, 'it should never have happened – I'd had a fight with my husband, and I had too much to drink…'

He took her hand. 'You don't have to make excuses. It did happen, and it was great. If you're embarrassed about it, well, you didn't *have* to see me again. I didn't call you back for that reason.'

She took another gulp of vodka. 'I just wanted to explain.' She hesitated and then rushed on. 'I just didn't want to leave you with the wrong impression of me.'

'You left me with a beautiful impression. Your perfume was all over my bed, and the smell of your body, and the way you cried out when you came.' He reached over for her and she halfheartedly tried to pull away. But their mouths met and she was lost. He was young and full of strength, and this time she was almost sober. His whole feeling seemed to be to try to please her, and in return she found herself twice as adept at thrilling him. They made love for a long time, and it was very very good. Afterward they lay and talked.

She felt so peaceful and protected by him. He listened quietly while she told him about David and his indifference toward her. She told him everything about herself, about the children, about her life. They smoked cigarettes and drank more vodka.

She found out about him too. He was an artist. He had left art school a year before and was now working as assistant to the art editor of a glossy women's magazine. The paintings on the wall were all his. She found out they were of an ex-girlfriend called Margarethe.

It was a sad story. They met at art school and fell in love. After living together for six months they decided to get married. Paul's mother was dead and his father, a retired businessman, lived in Cheltenham. He took Margarethe to meet father. She met father, and three days later she married him.

Paul was stunned; he couldn't believe it. He had a terrible fight with both of them and hadn't seen or heard from them since.

'I couldn't accept it,' he said. 'I don't believe she could have loved him. I suppose she wanted his money. I couldn't offer her any security.'

'How do you feel about her now?' questioned Linda.

'I don't know,' he said moodily. 'She's a bitch. They just went off one afternoon and came back married.'

'Why do you still keep your paintings of her around?'

He shrugged. 'Just to remind me not to be such a jerk again. I can't make it with girls anymore, y'know. Maybe once or twice, then I just don't want to know.'

She remembered whiny-voiced, pretty little Melanie.

'I imagine I'm all right because I'm married?' she guessed.

'I think you're great.'

They lay in silence for a while, both mulling over their problems.

'The thing that really gets me,' he said, 'is imagining Margarethe living in Cheltenham with my old man. She was such a swinger. She liked to ball more than anyone I ever knew. I just can't see her fancying him. He's so old.'

'What was your mother like?'

'It's a long story.'

She leaned over and kissed him lightly on the forehead.

'Tell me about it,' she said gently.

'You sound like a psychiatrist,' he laughed. 'Actually, it's a *lousy* story. She killed herself when I was fifteen.'

Linda was shocked. She wanted to ask why – but Paul had turned over on his side and closed his eyes. 'It's a drag,' he muttered. 'I'll tell you about it some other time.'

After a while she looked at her watch, and seeing that it was past eleven said, 'Look, I had better be leaving. David's going to be home at twelve.'

'Why don't you stay the night?' he mumbled, his back still to her.

'I'd like to, but I just can't not be there when he gets home – he knows I never stay out – he'd probably call the police.'

'It's funny, isn't it,' Paul said. 'All the little birds I bang and can't get rid of.' He put on a high thin voice. 'Oh, darling, let me stay the night – Mummy and Daddy never expect me before morning.' They both laughed. 'I tell you, it's horrible, they just will not go. And you know what it's like to screw someone and then not be able to stand them near you after. Y'know, Linda, you're the first female since Margarethe I've asked to stay the night – and you say no.'

She dressed slowly as Paul lay lazily back in bed watching her.

'Y'know, you're very sexy. I wouldn't mind seeing you in long black nylons and a black garter belt.'

'What would you do, take pictures?'

'No – I'd paint you – sort of lying on a sofa. *Very sexy*. Can I?'

'I'll think about it.' She laughed, slightly embarrassed. Eventually she was ready to go.

'When am I going to see you?' he asked.

'I don't know.'

'Tomorrow?'

'I don't know, Paul. It's very difficult for me to make plans.'

'You can't leave without telling me when.'

'I'll phone you in the morning.'

He gave her his phone number at work, kissed her long and hard, and she set off on her journey home. It was eleven-thirty.

Chapter Nine

Claudia left the restaurant in a fury. She hailed a taxi and directed it to Conrad Lee's hotel. She was fed up with David Cooper. Stupid bastard – just who did he think he was? At first their affair had been fun. She enjoyed affairs with married men, they were a race apart, and always a challenge. Also, she had misguidedly thought he might be able to help her career.

Nothing. He had done absolutely nothing. Being Miss Beauty Maid appeared to lead to a dead end. He hadn't even given her a decent present, just a lot of unkept promises. So where was the famous mink jacket she was supposed to get? She didn't want money from him. How dare he offer her money like some cheap whore. But presents were a different matter.

'Cheapskate,' she muttered under her breath. He had even complained about picking up the check in the restaurant.

The taxi pulled up at the hotel, and a doorman leaped forward to escort her in.

She strolled coolly over to reception. 'I'd like to speak to Mr. Conrad Lee.'

They put her through on the house phone. After a while the operator said there was no reply.

'Would you try the phone in the bedroom, please,' she said.

The phone rang several times before it was picked up. 'Yeah?' His voice was thick and unfriendly.

'Conrad, this is Claudia Parker.'

'Who?'

'Claudia Parker,' she repeated patiently. 'You can't have forgotten last night already.'

There was a short pause, then, 'Oh, yeah, of course. How are you, baby? What can I do for you?'

'Your secretary called me earlier about seeing you tomorrow night. I was out with this dreary guy, and I suddenly thought the hell with it, what about tonight.'

He laughed, coughed unattractively, and said, 'Listen, baby, I'm all tied up tonight.'

'Oh.' She sounded disappointed. 'Look, I'm very adaptable. I never find three a crowd.'

'Do you mean what I think you mean?' he questioned.

'Of course I do,' she purred. 'You were so fantastic last night, I don't mind sharing.'

'Hang on a minute,' Conrad said, and the phone was muffled. She waited patiently, and soon his voice came back full of interest. 'Come right on up. We'll be waiting.'

She hung up, smiling, and made her way leisurely to the powder room, where for the next twenty minutes she touched up her makeup and rearranged her hair so that it fell around her shoulders thick and shiny. She looked very gorgeous, young, sexy and pretty. Her figure was shown off to its best advantage in the low-cut black dress she was wearing.

A half-hour had passed by the time she finally knocked on the door of his suite.

He answered it immediately – wearing a green-and-orange-striped bathrobe. 'Where the fuck have you been?' he demanded.

She smiled apologetically, walked into the living room and sat down, crossing her legs carefully to be sure there was the maximum amount of thigh showing. She knew she looked great.

'I'm so sorry,' she said. 'I know you're going to think I'm terrible. But what I said on the phone about a threesome and everything. Well, I am sorry, but I just can't.'

He stared at her disbelievingly. 'You can't?' he said thickly.

She shook her head slowly, fluttering long black eyelashes. 'I guess I wanted to see you again so much that I said it – but really, it's not my scene.'

'It's not your scene,' he repeated blankly.

'No.' She licked her lips, crossed her legs the other way, and waited.

'Look, baby,' he said at last, 'you called me while I was balling this chick' – he indicated the bedroom – 'you called *me,* right in the middle. Nobody asked you to, but there you were on the phone, asking, and I mean asking, to join us. So what happens – you get me all hot over the idea of a scene – I stop halfway with this other broad, wait a goddam half-hour, and then you mince in here saying you can't make it.' His voice had been rising excitedly, and now he was almost screaming.

She stood up. 'What can I say?' She walked over to him and put her hand on his arm. 'I was drunk last night, but in spite of that I remembered it as something special. Now I'm sober, and can I help it if I don't want to share you?'

He looked at her admiringly. 'You're a smart little cookie. I suppose you want me to get rid of—' He gestured toward the bedroom.

She kissed him, pressing herself up against him. 'That's the general idea.'

He pushed her away. 'All right, baby – but don't think you're fooling me, because I know exactly what you're doing. You happen to be a lot sexier than her, so I'll pay her off. Is that what you want?'

She looked at him wide-eyed. 'I don't know what you're talking about,' she said. 'Do whatever you like. I'll still be available tomorrow night. I can always go now.'

His eyes swept over her body. 'No, you stay. Wait in the john.'

She smiled and walked obediently into the guest bathroom, in the hall. He kept her waiting about five minutes. Soon she heard a shrieky female voice, and then a door slammed.

Eventually he threw open the bathroom door – he had discarded his vibrant bathrobe and stood there with nothing but his suntan and a hard-on. 'Let's go, baby,' he said. 'I just had to give that broad fifty bucks, so you'd better make it worth my while!'

* * *

David parked his car in the garage and let himself into the house. It was strangely quiet. He supposed Linda had gone to bed early, so he made his way upstairs and looked in on the children, who both slept peacefully. Jane woke up and sleepily requested a glass of water. He got it for her, and she threw her arms around his neck and said, 'I love you, Daddy.' He settled her down and went into the main bedroom.

It was empty. He was mildly surprised. Where was Linda? He knew the rest of the house was deserted. She must have gone to a movie or something, but it was most unlike her.

He checked through the window and saw her car was not in the drive, and then he looked around for a note – no note.

He went along to Ana's room and knocked. The maid came to the door clutching her transparent nylon nightdress around her. She had an unfortunate shadow of a moustache.

'Where's Mrs. Cooper?' he questioned.

'She went out maybe eight o'clock,' said Ana. Her English was not too good, and she didn't volunteer any further information.

'Did she say where she was going?'

'No.'

'What time she would be back?'

'No.'

The conversation was finished.

He went back to the bedroom, showered, and fell asleep reading the papers on the bed.

That was how Linda found him when she came in. She was agitated, he had said twelve o'clock, and he was always later than he said he would be. Fortunately he was asleep, as her makeup was smudged and her hair a mess. She knew if he saw her he would know. She made it into the bathroom quickly, got out of her clothes and into a robe. Then she ran a bath. At least if he woke up now it wouldn't matter.

David awoke. 'Where the hell have you been?' he demanded.

'I went to a movie. Where were you?'

'You know where I was. The movies get out at quarter to eleven – where have *you* been for the last hour?'

'I suppose you were with Phillip,' she said, ignoring his question.

'Yes – you know I was.'

'I was with him too.'

He stared at her blankly. 'What are you talking about?'

'I was with Phillip as much as you were.'

'Have you been drinking?'

'No, David, I haven't been drinking. I called the Abbottson house after speaking to you earlier, and while I was talking to Mary, Phillip came in and he knew nothing about a meeting with you.'

David thought quickly. 'Yes, things were a bit of a mess. I thought he was coming back later, but then I realized he said he couldn't, so I had to take those people from out of town to dinner.'

She raised an eyebrow. 'But you just *said* you were with Phillip.'

'Yes – well, that was because I knew you wouldn't understand.'

'You were right, I *don't* understand. Now, please, can I take a bath?'

'You're so ridiculous, Linda.' His voice was becoming louder. 'Look, I've been home for hours. I took these three men to Carlo's, and I ran into Jay and Lori Grossman. *Now* do you believe me? They want us to have dinner with them tomorrow, and I said it was all right. You can ask *them* who I was with. OK?'

Maybe he was telling the truth. 'Oh, all right,' she said wearily. She was too tired to fight.

He stalked back into the bedroom. She took her bath. Their thoughts were on separate planes. Neither of them really wanted to get involved in long discussions about who had been where, as it was dangerous ground and they could both end up getting found out.

When she came to bed he thought how good she looked in a long silk nightdress which clung seductively.

He broke the silence. 'Where would you like to eat tomorrow?'

She was noncommittal. 'I don't mind.'

'Jay says Lori wants to go to the Savoy Grill – a bit conventional, but I suppose as they are visitors here we should oblige.'

'I suppose so.' She turned out the light on her side of the bed and lay with her back toward him.

'What's new with the children?'

'Oh, nothing much.'

He lit a cigarette. 'I'm not tired,' he remarked.

'Why don't you read? There's a book on the table you started three months ago.'

'I don't feel like reading.'

'Then turn your light off and go to sleep.'

'That's a pretty nightdress. Is it new?'

'No, I've been wearing it for the past two years,' she sighed patiently, wishing he would just shut up.

He leaned over and cupped her left breast with his hand. She shrank away immediately. Oh, God, no, she thought, not tonight – please God, not tonight. After all those nights I've lain here and ached for him, he couldn't possibly pick tonight.

He lunged across the bed after her. 'What's the matter?'

'Nothing.' She forced herself to turn around and face him.

Fortunately he took her quickly. He had long ago given up on preliminaries with her. The sexual act with David gave her absolutely no pleasure. She felt vacant and used. Vaguely she wondered if all men became like this after you married them. At first anxious to please, thrilled to bits if they got to fondle you for half an hour. But after the marriage – a quick lay and that was all.

'That was marvellous,' he said. 'How was it for you?'

She simulated pleasure. 'Marvellous.' She repeated his adjective, unable to think of anything else to say.

He turned the light out. 'Good night.'

She squeezed her eyes shut to keep in the tears. 'Good night.'

He lay there and thought about what a bitch Claudia was.

She lay there and thought about how virile and sensitive Paul was.

Finally they both fell asleep.

Chapter Ten

'I want to stay the night,' Claudia said, stretching languorously.

Conrad was on the phone to room service. He sat on the side of the bed, rolls of suntanned flesh around his middle, his bald head shining with sweat.

'This is Mr. Lee, suite 206 – send me up six pieces of lightly buttered toast spread with caviar, the best stuff. Also a bucket of ice, a glass of milk, and a dish of chocolate ice cream.' He glanced over at Claudia – 'You want anything, baby?'

She shook her head.

He spoke into the phone again. 'Add on some chocolate cake and cream – a jug of cream. OK, that's all. Make it fast!'

'I'm going to stay the night,' Claudia announced.

'What do you want to do that for?'

''Cos I want to go to the studio with you tomorrow like you promised. I'm not letting you out of my sight!'

He laughed. 'Baby, you're too much! I've been married three times, and I thought I knew broads pretty well, but you're something else!'

She laughed too, throwing her head back so that her hair spread out around her. 'Wouldn't you sooner I was honest?' she asked. 'I'm not some naïve little piece, you know. I like you. But I don't see why you shouldn't help me.'

'I haven't promised you anything.'

'Yes, you have, you promised me a test.'

'So I promised you a test. So what if you're lousy?'

'I won't be lousy.' She smiled. 'I may not be able to act, but I photograph like a dream! And in the sort of movie you're making, I'm sure you can find something for me.'

There was a discreet knock on the bedroom door. 'Your order is here, sir,' a voice said.

Conrad lumbered off the bed and reached for a paisley silk dressing gown.

God – you're old and fat, Claudia thought. 'I love your dressing gown, darling,' she purred.

'Simpson's,' he said, pleased. He grabbed some change off the dressing table and disappeared into the other room.

Claudia rolled across the bed, twining herself around in the sheet. 'I'm going to get in his damn movie if it kills me,' she muttered to herself. 'I haven't screwed *that* for nothing!'

He came back into the bedroom munching on a piece of toast. 'This is lousy caviar – you want to go out somewhere?'

'What time is it?' she asked, surprised.

He consulted a large gold watch. 'One-thirty – what's open?'

She thought quickly. If they went out she wanted to be sure that she came back to the hotel with him after. She was determined to stick with him until he got her a test.

'All the clubs stay open till around four,' she said. 'And we can stop by my apartment so I can get some clothes to wear to the studio tomorrow. Great idea.' She jumped out of bed.

He studied her figure. 'You know, you've got a gorgeous body. How would you feel about appearing on the screen nude?'

'I hadn't really thought about it.'

'Think about it. There's a part you might be right for. I can test you.'

'When?' Her green eyes gleamed.

They went to a new discotheque – Charlie Brown's. It was jammed, but they were squeezed onto an already full table due to the fact that Conrad slipped the headwaiter money. The music was so loud you couldn't hear yourself speak. On the tiny dance floor couples were jammed frantically together. There was a scattering of well-known people, a lot of girls with long straight hair covering half their faces, and a few representatives of the latest rock groups sporting hair as long as the girls'. It was very dark.

At their table was a photographer Claudia knew. She greeted him with a kiss and introduced him to Conrad. He was with one of the top models of the moment, a tall slim girl who photographed out of this world.

Claudia couldn't sit still; the music swept over her in great waves.

'Want to dance?' she asked Conrad.

He nodded and they struggled to the dance floor, where she broke loose in wild sinuous gyrations while Conrad just sort of stood there jiggling about. It was hot and the sweat started to trickle down his face.

You think you're a real swinger, Claudia thought. Don't you know you're too old to do this?

She said, 'Darling, you're a peachy dancer!'

'Sweetie pie!' The voice was unmistakable. Right beside them on the dance floor was Shirley, complete with the Honourable Jeremy. 'Where's your divine boyfriend?'

Claudia smiled. 'Thought you were going to Windsor,' she yelled.

'We did, but it was absolutely *too* dreadful. I mean, it was almost empty. Can you imagine anything more ghastly?'

The Honourable Jeremy nodded vehement agreement.

By this time Conrad was sweating profusely. 'Let's sit down,' he said weakly.

'Sweetie, we will come over in a minute. Where are you sitting?'

Claudia smiled and waved, pretending she hadn't heard. She didn't relish the thought of being stuck with Shirley and Jeremy again.

When they got back to their table it was even more crowded, and there was a great squeezing up of people to make room for them.

The model said to Conrad, 'I adored your last film. Will you be making your new one in this country?'

The photographer asked Claudia to dance. She accepted, not too eager to leave the skinny model chatting up Conrad, but anxious to dance again, and Giles, the photographer, was a wild dancer. She had indulged in a short affair with him at one time, but then they decided it was more fun to be mates. They were too much of a kind to be lovers. Occasionally, if one of them was at a loose end, they would call each other and spend an evening together, and if they felt like it, end up in bed. But it was purely a brother-and-sister relationship with a little sex thrown in. Giles was very good-looking in a dark Spanish way. Women were mad for him, and his services as a fashion and society photographer were in demand.

'Who's the father figure?' he asked cynically. 'Cindy says he's a big Hollywood mogul, and I think she fancies big Hollywood moguls.'

'You can tell her to keep her false nails off this one, he's already been bagged!'

They did a ritual dance together – him standing very still and giving rhythmic sexy twitches and she almost bumping and grinding before him.

'Fancy a bit of pot?' he asked conversationally.

She glanced over at their table. More people had joined it, and Conrad seemed quite happy ordering drinks and talking loudly with a lot of arm-waving.

'Yeah, great idea,' she said.

They slipped off the dance floor and out onto a balcony that extended along one-half of the club. It was windy and surprisingly quiet, as the windows and doors from the club were all soundproofed.

Giles lit a joint and they took it in turns to drag deeply on it.

'I've got to get in the right frame of mind to screw that bag of bones,' he said. 'We're doing a big layout for *Vogue,* and I want to have the right atmosphere between us. Christ, I tell you, it's like banging a skeleton!'

They both giggled. 'Lots of luck,' laughed Claudia. 'How would you like mine? Attractive, isn't he?'

'I'd suggest a foursome,' said Giles, 'but I know we'd only end up doing it to each other, so what's the use?'

They both collapsed in gales of laughter, then Claudia said, 'C'mon, we'd better get back inside.'

'What's the scene?' Giles asked. 'You going to become a big movie starlet?'

'Star – baby – star.'

They walked back into the noise and heat and rejoined their table. Cindy was listening attentively as Conrad told a long boring story about how he first arrived in America at the age of fourteen. Shirley and the Honourable Jeremy had also squeezed around the table.

'Sweetie – what a fascinating man!' gasped Shirley. 'Such a history!' She simpered at Giles. 'Hello, poppet.'

'Hello, Shirley – how's business?'

'Business?'

He laughed. 'Forget it, baby.'

'I say, old man,' stammered Jeremy, 'liked those photos you did of Shirley – jolly fine set.'

'I'm a jolly fine photographer,' mocked Giles.

Claudia decided it was about time she came between Cindy's adoring gaze and Conrad. She snaked her arm around his neck and whispered something in his ear.

He looked surprised. 'Here?' he said. 'Now?'

She giggled. 'No one will see. Want me to?'

He laughed hoarsely. 'You're a wild broad. Save it for later, huh?'

Conrad ordered champagne for the whole table, and everyone proceeded to get well and truly loaded. 'I'm going to throw a big party tomorrow night,' he said.

Claudia was delighted. 'For me, darling?'

'Yeah, for you – anyone – you're all invited.'

'Oh, goodie – how super,' trilled Shirley. 'Where and what time, sweetie?'

'Make it at my hotel – Plaza Carlton – I'll take over a big room there – about ten o'clock.'

'Crazy,' said Claudia. 'Did everybody hear that – tomorrow at ten.' She kissed Conrad's ear. 'I'm just going to the loo – be right back.' She threaded her way through the crowded tables to reception. 'I want to make a quick phone call,' she said to the girl behind the desk.

'Go ahead,' said the girl passing over the house phone.

It was after three o'clock. She dialled the number slowly, a strange smile playing around her lips.

A sleepy voice answered the phone.

'Hello, David darling,' she whispered. 'I'm having a great time. How about you?' She hung up immediately. 'Just letting my husband know everything's cool,' she said to the surprised girl and swept back inside.

* * *

Waking up the next morning was not too much fun. Seeing Conrad asleep beside her like a discontented slug made her stomach turn. Her head felt heavy and her skin like much-used parchment. She made it to the bathroom and took an icy-cold shower. It was absolutely freezing agony, but the after-effects were worth it.

They had not returned to Conrad's hotel earlier that morning but instead had ended up in her apartment.

After the shower she dressed carefully and did a meticulous makeup, all ready to accompany Conrad to the studio. Then she made some coffee and finally shook him.

99

He awoke badly. Much coughing and foul sounds in his throat, bloodshot eyes, bad breath and BO. 'Christ, what time is it?' he muttered, the universal cry of people waking up in other people's apartments.

'It's just ten o'clock.' She handed him some coffee.

'Where's the phone?'

She groped around under the bed, where she had placed the phone off the hook.

He called his secretary and issued a list of instructions. 'I've got to go back to the hotel and get changed,' he said, struggling into his clothes.

'I'm coming with you.'

'What for?'

'For my test you promised me.'

He stared at her. 'I'm not going to forget your goddamn test – but it can't be done just like that, today. It's got to be set up.'

'I'll come with you while you set it up.'

He shook his head. 'You don't give up, do you?' He picked up the phone and called his secretary again. 'Listen. I want a test fixed for a Miss Claudia—' He looked at her blankly.

'Parker,' she said quickly.

'Parker. Fix it up as soon as possible. Her agent will call you later today to get the details.' He hung up. 'OK, baby?'

She kissed him. 'You bet! Listen, you haven't forgotten the party tonight?'

'Party?'

'Yes. Don't you remember? You asked a whole group of people to a party tonight at your hotel.'

'Oh, yeah – that's right. I'll get it in hand, and I'll see you later.'

'I'll come by a couple of hours early in case you need anything.'

'The way I feel right now, I won't need anything – but you never know.' He gave a ribald laugh and left.

Chapter Eleven

Linda phoned Paul at work as soon as the children had gone to school and David to the office. He was anxious to see her.

'I can't manage it,' she said.

He was most persuasive and eventually she agreed to meet him during his lunch hour.

It was a crisp sunny day, and they met in Green Park. She had never seen him in a suit before, and it didn't look quite right somehow. She decided it was because it was off the rack and store-bought suits always managed to look just that little bit wrong.

They strolled along hand in hand, but Linda didn't feel easy. She felt overdressed in her smart outfit with matching crocodile shoes and bag. She knew she looked all wrong strolling hand in hand with Paul Bedford in Green Park. It wasn't that she felt old, or at least older than him – but she felt, in spite of the fact that she didn't want to feel that way – she felt as if she was slumming.

'What's on your mind?' he asked. 'Something bothering you?'

'I don't know, Paul. This is all wrong. I'm not the sort of woman that can get involved in an affair. I have my children and my home, and I feel I have to keep trying with my husband. I can't just give up and become involved with you. That's no answer at all.'

He was irritated. 'What's the matter, Linda? Frightened of losing your security if David finds out?'

'No. I'm frightened of losing my self-respect.'

They walked in silence for a while and then he said, 'What are you trying to say?'

'I'm trying to say that I can't lead two lives. I want to stop it now before it goes any further.'

His voice sounded bleak. 'I don't want you to leave me. I've been waiting to meet someone like you. You're a warm person. I *need* a warm person. I won't make any demands on you, just to see you when you're free.'

'It's not enough for either of us. I don't think we should see each other again.' She withdrew her hand.

His mood changed. 'You're like all the others. I should have known you're just a hard bitch at heart, frightened of losing all your home comforts. Women have hearts like bloody adding machines. Look at Margarethe – dropped me for my father just because he had a few bob. My bloody mother killed herself to get away from him. Fuck the lot of you.'

'I'm sorry, Paul – but I'm not going to be a substitute for your mother or Margarethe. I'm too old for that. Forget the past and go and find someone you can be happy with.'

'Is that what you want?'

'Yes. It is.'

He sneered at her. 'Well, you were a bloody easy lay – and not bad for an old bird.'

She turned and started to walk quickly away.

'Who's going to screw you now, you randy bitch!' he yelled after her.

She felt the colour rise in her face, and started to run, not stopping until she reached her car.

She drove home, cold tears running down her face all the way.

The Grossmans were sitting in the bar of their hotel, Lori cool in pale-lilac chiffon, silver hair swept back in elaborate curls, neckline plunging to show off two satin-smooth white breasts.

The Coopers arrived to meet them on time. Linda was wearing a black silk dress and pale-beige mink wrap. David, conventional in a midnight-blue suit, white shirt, blue tie, and big sapphire cufflinks.

They all had a drink and then moved on to the Savoy Grill.

Jay enlivened the evening with amusing tales about Hollywood. David chatted amicably about business and politics. The two women were mostly silent. Lori was obviously disappointed that Princess Margaret wasn't there. She complained about the lack of ice and checked her makeup a lot.

Jay finally said, 'For Christ's sake, stop looking in the mirror. We all know you're beautiful. It's the reason I married you, isn't it?'

She pouted a lot after that.

When they were at the coffee stage Jay said, 'Hey – how about dropping by the party Conrad's giving tonight? We promised we would.'

'I'm really tired,' Linda said apologetically. 'It was the children's first day at school and what with all the preparation I'm rather exhausted.'

'Come on, Linda,' said David jovially, 'we'll go for an hour.' He was feeling rather pleased with himself due to the fact that he had avoided getting in touch with Claudia all day. Little tramp, teach her a lesson. And how about that, phoning him up in the middle of the night to make him jealous? He would show *her.* She would have to come begging to be forgiven.

'Yes, Linda, you must come,' said Jay. 'It will be a laugh, I can promise you that.'

'Just for an hour then,' she said reluctantly.

She accompanied Lori to the ladies' room, where between applying powder and blusher Lori drawled, 'That son of a bitch thinks I'm a damn idiot. He'll find out who's the idiot when I get half of everything he's got.'

'I beg your pardon?' said Linda politely.

'It's California law – I *know* it's California law.' At that Lori sank into silence, carefully applying another coat of lip gloss.

The party was in full swing when they arrived. There were sixty or seventy people there already, and more arriving all the time. A huge buffet of food covered one side of the room, with three bars strategically placed, and a six-piece live group to which people were dancing.

They pushed their way through to the nearest bar and ordered drinks. Jay appeared to know quite a few people. He introduced everybody, and soon David was chatting away.

'Come with me to find Conrad,' Jay said to Linda. 'I've got to let him know I put in an appearance.'

They found Conrad sitting at a table eating chocolate ice cream and drinking straight bourbon. Claudia was by his side – wearing a bright-red ruffled dress and a lot of fake diamonds.

Conrad issued genial greetings and invited them to sit down, moving two other people to do so.

'You remember Mrs. Cooper – Linda,' Jay said.

'Sure, sure. What do you think of the party? I know how to do these things right, huh?'

'You certainly do,' Jay said admiringly.

'Hallo, Mrs. Cooper,' Claudia said, slurring her words. She had been drinking steadily for several hours. 'Is *Mr* Cooper about?'

'Why, yes,' said Linda. 'Did you want to see him about something?'

'Yes, as a matter of fact I do.' She knocked a glass down on the table accidentally, the dark alcohol making a splashy stain on the tablecloth. 'I want to tell him what he can do with his bloody Beauty Maid campaign. Stuff it up his ass – that's what he can do with it.' She hiccuped.

Linda stared at her coolly. 'I'll see he gets the message, dear.' She turned to talk to Jay.

Claudia stood up. 'Think I'll give him the bloody message myself,' she said and weaved unsteadily off.

'What's the matter with her?' Linda said.

Jay shrugged. 'I don't know. What's with your girlfriend, Con?'

Conrad laughed. 'The broad's nutty. I've promised her a bit in the movie. It's gone to her head.'

'What bit?'

'How about a semi-naked broad standing beside the credits, sort of torn-slave-dress jazz. This kid's got a great body – and if she photographs OK, we'll use her. Whattayasay?'

'Fine,' said Jay with a smile. 'Sounds like it has a lot of class.'

Linda rose from the table. 'Excuse me a minute,' she said. She walked around the room looking for David, but she couldn't find him or the girl. She sighed. It was probably nothing – the girl was drunk.

She spotted Lori surrounded by a group of admiring males and went over.

Lori was saying, 'Well, where I come from women are treated like ladies. You see—'

'Have you seen David?' Linda interrupted.

'Yeah.' She hardly glanced at Linda. 'He went out on the terrace.'

It's stupid, Linda thought. I shouldn't be tracking him down like this, it's childish. She made her way onto the terrace and found it deserted.

Just as she was leaving, she heard a low, throaty chuckle. She looked again and saw over in the corner a couple in a close embrace.

She backed into the shadows and edged nearer. The girl was pulling his head down to her breast, which was popping out of the top of her dress. She was fondling him intimately.

'You're the craziest, Claudia,' he muttered. 'The best ever.' Now he was pulling her dress right down so it hung around her waist. 'I missed you so much. One night without having you was murder.'

Shocked and sickened, Linda backed away. They hadn't seen her. Dazed, she wandered back into the main room.

She was heading for the door when Jay appeared and grabbed her arm. 'What's the matter? You look terrible. What happened?'

She looked at him with unseeing eyes. 'I've got to get out of here,' she mumbled, pushing his arm away and making for the door.

He caught hold of her arm again firmly and steered her to the nearest bar.

'The lady wants a large brandy, and fast,' he said. 'Now, tell me what happened.' He took her hand and held it tight. 'Tell me,' he repeated in a softer voice.

She looked at him with eyes full of shock. 'I suspected he played around – maybe – once in a while up in Manchester or somewhere, but this… With me right here. It's horrible.'

The waiter brought the brandy, and she took large gulps.

'I – I was looking for David. I wanted to warn him about that drunk tramp. Lori said he was on the terrace. I went out and he was there with her. They were necking – she had half her dress off. They were saying these things to each other…'

'Oh, God!' said Jay. 'That stupid son of a bitch. Look – the girl was drunk. Maybe he was trying to get rid of her.'

Linda's eyes were scornful. 'With words like – "one night without having you was murder"?'

'What do you want to do?' asked Jay. 'Shall I take you home?'

She shook her head. 'What *can* I do? This is it for me. I'm finished with him. I want a divorce. I hate him.' Her voice shook. 'I don't ever want to speak to him again.'

'Look – it's no good making decisions while you're upset. Let me take you home. I'll come straight back and talk to David, tell him not to go home tonight.'

She laughed bitterly. 'Tell him not to ever come home again. Tell him to go off with his "best-ever" little slut. Tell him he can do what he wants – 'cos I don't care anymore. I'm through.' She took another large gulp of brandy. 'I'm going to start crying in a minute – please get me out of here.'

They got a taxi outside the hotel. Linda was worried that either Lori or David would miss them and that maybe David would race her home, but Jay reassured her. 'I'll be back within an hour, and if he does miss you he'll just be looking around. As for Lori, she won't even know I'm gone.'

Linda sighed. 'I'm so embarrassed, dragging you away from the party and everything. The whole situation is so awful.'

'Don't be embarrassed.' He took her hand comfortingly. 'If it's any solace I was involved in exactly the same situation myself. In Hollywood at a real swinging party, my first wife, Jenny, vanished. I searched all over and eventually found her in bed with the host. So you see, I *do* understand.'

'What did *you* do?'

'I was a schmuck. I gave her another chance. Came home early one day and found her banging the delivery boy.'

They sat in silence for a while, then Jay said, 'I suppose for some people one woman or one man is enough – but not for any of the people I know. I guess one gets what one deserves out of life. I've been married three times – each time to a beautiful girl with about as much thinking power as a rabbit. It must be a sickness with me – I marry stupid, dumb, beautiful broads.'

Linda hesitated. 'I – I was unfaithful to David this week. The first time in eleven years of marriage. I'm so ashamed about it now. It was with a boy – a twenty-two-year-old boy – I don't know why…' She trailed off. 'David hadn't touched me in months. We were so far apart, he was never home. It just happened. I suppose I'm as guilty as he is.'

'Never feel guilty. What good can that do? Sleep on things, and see how you feel in the morning. You've got young children – don't make any hasty decisions.'

'Good night, Jay – thank you for everything.'

'Linda, I'll call you tomorrow. Rest easy – it will be all right.'

* * *

Claudia found David in a group with Lori. She edged quietly up behind him, and pressing her body against his back, she covered his eyes with her hands and said in a Marilyn Monroe-type voice, 'Guess who, baby!'

There was no mistaking that body. He was surprised and sharply excited. She had the most incredible effect on him: he just had to know she was there to want her. He turned slowly, eyes looking around to see if Linda was anywhere about. She wasn't.

'Hello, Claudia.'

'Hello, Claudia.' She mimicked his voice. 'Don't I get a better greeting than that? By the way, you can stuff your Beauty Maid campaign up your ass, cha-cha-cha!'

The group he had been standing with were all listening, including Lori.

He took Claudia firmly by the arm, bruising her flesh. 'Let's go and find Linda,' he said, walking off and pulling her with him.

'Let's go find Linda!' she said incredulously. 'You've got to be joking!'

He marched her onto the terrace, finding a deserted dark corner. As soon as he let go of her she wound her arms around his neck and kissed him. 'Did you miss me?' she whispered. 'I was going to be so mad at you, but I couldn't.' She giggled. 'I'm smashed, you know.'

'You're a bitch, leaving me sitting in that restaurant, phoning up in the middle of the night. *You* were going to be mad? What about *me?*'

She nibbled his ear, rubbing her body against him.

Her dress was held up by two thin shoulder straps. He peeled them off, pulling her dress down to her waist. She wore nothing underneath. Hungrily she guided his mouth to her breasts.

All sense of reason was gone. He was with Claudia and he had to have her. It didn't matter that they were in a public place. That his wife was somewhere around. That anybody could appear.

It was dark. He pushed her down onto the cold concrete ground and lifted her skirt. She wore no panties, and she was giggling.

He took her quickly. It was all over in a minute.

'Christ!' he muttered. 'Christ!'

She lay there still giggling, her dress bunched around her waist. He pulled her up and looked around, relieved to see that no one had come out. She was unconcerned.

'We've got to go back inside separately,' he said.

'Screw you!' she replied.

'You just did.' He straightened his tie and wiped a handkerchief around his face to remove all traces of lipstick. 'I'll phone you tomorrow. I'll get away early from the office and come over. I've got a surprise for you.'

'You've always got a surprise for me. You're the man with the permanent hard-on!' She laughed. 'What a title for a television series – I can see it now – The Man with the Permanent Hard-on – starring Dick Hampton!'

He kissed her. 'You go in first – go straight to the ladies' room, you look a mess.'

'Thank you, kind sir. Are you sure you're finished with me?'

'Go on, be a good girl. I'll try to phone you later.'

She stuck out her tongue at him – waggling it obscenely – and then sauntered off through the French windows completely at ease.

He took a deep breath – what a girl. After a safe five minutes he followed her in. The party was still in full swing. He grabbed a drink from a passing waiter and started to look for Linda. This was becoming a dangerous habit, bumping into Claudia at parties.

He observed Lori dancing with a seedy actor. She was moving her hips in steady bumps and grinds, and smiled coolly at him. She certainly knew how to move.

He edged closer. 'Seen Linda?' he asked.

She looked deadpan. 'Last I saw of her she was heading toward the terrace looking for you.'

'The terrace?' he said, stunned.

'The terrace, honey.' She swayed away from him.

He started to look for Linda seriously. He ploughed his way across the room, through groups of people laughing and chatting. A girl grabbed his arm. She was thin and pretty, and he remembered her as a friend of Claudia's from the restaurant.

'Hello, ducky,' she cooed. 'Fancy seeing you here.'

'Hello.' He looked around for her chinless boyfriend.

'Oh, Jeremy's gone to fetch me another drink.' She didn't leave go of his arm. 'Super party – but I didn't expect you to be here.'

'Why not?' he said patiently. She was far too thin for him to find attractive.

'I know we're all very modern and everything, but you struck me as the jealous type.'

'What are you talking about?' He shook his arm free.

'After all – this party is being given by Conrad Lee for Claudia, and I shouldn't have thought you would come. I mean, one shouldn't mix business with pleasure, should one? And you're obviously pleasure, and he's obviously business.' She smiled blandly. 'Here comes Jeremy with my drink. See you again,' and she walked off.

He stood there, furious.

Claudia hadn't mentioned Conrad Lee or the fact that the party was for her. Bitch! Bitch! Bitch!

The quest for Linda was forgotten, and a new one for Claudia began. He wanted to get a few facts straight.

* * *

Jay arrived back at the party. He was thoughtful. It was a tricky situation telling another man he couldn't go home to his own wife. It could easily end in a punch on the nose. He saw David across the room talking to a girl. David Cooper. An attractive man, big and dark, and the ladies all fell for him. Lori had said she thought he was probably fantastic in bed, but from talking to Linda it didn't sound that way. Lori had a habit of thinking most men were fantastic in bed, her way of letting him know that she didn't think *he* was.

He approached David quickly – best to get it over with fast – and told him the situation.

David was suitably flattened. He tried to deny it, but when Jay told him word for word what Linda had said, he was forced to admit it.

'You're an idiot,' Jay said. 'You've got a great wife. If you want to fuck around, why do it under her nose?'

'What is she going to do?'

'She mentioned divorce.'

'That's ridiculous. She's got no proof. So I kissed a girl at a party – what does that prove? I'm going home. I'm not going to be shut out of my own house.'

Jay shrugged. 'I can't stop you, I can only offer advice. She's in a state of shock. Going home tonight will only make things worse. If you wait until morning I'm sure you'll both see things a lot clearer.'

'I know Linda. She's upset, but I can explain things to her.'

Jay glared at him. 'I promised her you'd stay away tonight.'

David glared back. 'Tough, my friend, because I'm going home now.'

They held the glare a few moments and then Jay said, 'Good night, schmuck. Don't forget to say good night to your girlfriend. You'll probably find her kissing Conrad's ass.'

Chapter Twelve

When David arrived at his house and put the key in the front door, it wouldn't open. He lit a match to make sure he was using the right key, but although it turned smoothly, the door remained tightly shut. Realization dawned. Linda had bolted it from the inside.

He went around to the back door, but that was also tightly barred. A strong, choked anger rose in him. He returned to the front and pressed his finger firmly down on the bell push. The jangly sound of the buzzer was loud and insistent. There was no response. He tried it again, this time leaving his finger there for several minutes. A light went on in the upstairs window. It was the maid's room. He waited impatiently for her to come down and let him in, but nothing happened, and after a while her light went out again.

He was furious – Linda was obviously up and had told Ana to ignore the bell. He kicked savagely at the door but only succeeded in hurting his foot.

This is incredible, he thought. Who the fuck does she think the bloody house belongs to?

'Listen, Linda,' he shouted. 'Don't do this to me – open the door or I'm going for the police.'

The house loomed still and dark before him. He banged on the door with his fists – nothing. He leaned on the bell push again – nothing. Then, faintly, from upstairs there floated down the sound of a child crying. He stood there, undecided about what to do.

He felt guilty about waking the children, but after all, it was Linda's fault for not letting him in. He pushed the bell firmly and insistently for one final time, and to his surprise the bolts were pushed back and the door opened a few inches. He went to push it farther open but it clanged to a shuddering stop – held by the safety chain.

Linda peered out at him, white-faced and angry. 'Go away. You make me sick.' Her voice sounded flat and tired.

'Come *on,* let me in. We'll talk about it. It was nothing – I was drunk.'

'I don't want to talk to you. I don't want to see you. Go back to your little tramp and leave me alone.'

She slammed the door in his face.

He swore, hammered on the door, and shouted, 'You'll be sorry, Linda. I'll bloody go away and I won't come back!'

She didn't return. Furious, he strode back to his car, got in, and started it viciously.

* * *

When David left the party, Jay phoned Linda and warned her. He then got hold of Lori who was dancing closely with a swarthy-faced ambassador, and sat her down in a corner.

'You saw David take that broad out onto the terrace. What's with you, big mouth? Why did you tell Linda?'

She looked uninterested. 'I don't know what you're talking about, honey,' she drawled. 'Is something going on?'

'Yeah, something's going on.' He shrugged disgustedly. 'Are you really as dumb as you pretend to be?'

She looked sulky. 'You're so nasty to me, Jay. I don't know why I married you.'

'Would two mink coats, a sable, a mansion and several cars jog your memory?'

She stood up, smoothing her hands down her body, ironing imaginary wrinkles from her dress. 'I'm going to dance again. You interrupted me before – that was a very sweet, important guy I was dancing with.' She walked off, beautiful, cool.

Jay shook his head in despair. She was an idiot or a bitch or a clever combination of both.

The noise at the table where Conrad and his group were sitting was becoming progressively louder. Shrieks of drunken laughter, spilt drinks. Claudia climbing on the table and dancing, with the men all peering up her skirt, becoming aware of the fact that she had no panties on. Egged on with screams of drunken encouragement, she started to peel her dress off.

Jay viewed the scene. He was horribly sober. They all seemed to be behaving like a bunch of wild monkeys. He felt disgusted.

A large crowd was gathering around the table, goggle-eyed at Claudia's free show. The foreign ambassador rushed over with Lori. It was a fast striptease as Claudia only had her dress to take off. She kicked it from the table, and then proceeded to dance to the music. Bumping, grinding. Her body glistened proudly, and the men in the crowd pressed closer and closer while the women, suddenly jealous at such perfection, started to try and move them away.

A very harassed-looking man in pinstripe trousers and black jacket pushed his way toward the table. He represented the management. Shocked and horrified, he approached Conrad who waved him drunkenly away. 'We shall have to call the police unless this – this – woman gets dressed at once.'

Claudia stuck her tongue out at him, the only part of her that hadn't been exposed to public view.

Eventually, of course, the police arrived. They wrapped Claudia in a blanket, hauled her off to the police station, and booked her for indecent exposure.

The next morning it was headlines. Claudia was a star – for the day, that is. She was photographed and quoted while Conrad immediately cashed in on her wave of publicity by announcing that she would be appearing in his new film. He contacted her agent and signed her for two days' work.

She was delighted. She returned from the police station at lunch time, triumphant. She gave a press reception, posed for countless more pictures, and then was taken off to the studio in a chauffeured car for makeup and hair tests. She didn't see Conrad; efficient professionals took over. She was pleased – he had served his immediate purpose.

When she returned from the studio in the evening, David was propped outside her front door.

Sober and giddy with her sudden success, he didn't look so good to her. 'What do you want?' she said coldly, and then added with a burst of enthusiasm, 'Hey – did you see me in the papers today?'

He trailed her into the apartment and immediately fixed a drink.

She flitted around talking excitedly, forgetting her coldness of a moment before. After all, David did belong to someone else, and it was she he was coming to.

'I'm going to take you out to dinner tonight. Where do you want to go?' he asked.

She laughed. 'Oh. I see. All of a sudden I'm a star, and you want to be seen with me. What about wifey tonight? Aren't you frightened one of her spies will see us?'

'You don't have to worry about Linda. I've left her.'

Silence hung heavy in the room until slowly Claudia walked over and kissed him hard. 'You've left her for me?'

'For you.' He ran his hands down her back, enclosing them around her buttocks. 'When I saw you in the paper this morning and read what happened, I knew we couldn't go on any longer unless it was together. So I told Linda. I said I want a divorce, and here I am.'

She shook her head in disbelief. 'You really left her for me. Isn't that wild!'

'I'm going to divorce her and marry you,' he said firmly.

She wandered around the room. 'I don't want to get married, but thanks for the thought anyway. Hey, baby, we can do what we want, go where we want. It's too much!'

He followed her around the room. 'Don't you understand? I said I'd marry you.'

She laughed. 'But I don't want you to.'

'But I want to.' He grabbed hold of her. She was wearing a clingy orange sweater, matching slacks, and shiny white boots.

She slipped away from him. 'Listen, baby – let's get clear on the subject. I don't – do not have, I repeat, any desire to make the wedding-bells scene – so don't keep on making the offer like it's such a damn big deal. I don't want to marry you.' She was almost shouting, and sensing her mood, he dropped the subject.

'Where shall we go?' he said. 'We can go anywhere you like.'

She stretched, catlike in her orange outfit. 'I'm tired. I don't feel like getting dressed and going out.'

He looked surprised. 'You're always complaining we never go anywhere – and now that we can go wherever you like – you don't want to go.'

She flopped in a chair, her legs thrown casually over the side. 'Ever heard the story of the kid that wanted some candy – moaned and cried and carried on till eventually it got candy – then ate so much it was sick?' She giggled. 'Get the message?'

'What the hell's the matter with you? Don't you understand what I've done for you today?'

She shrugged. 'For me? I should have thought it would have been for yourself. Where are you going to live?'

'I'm taking an apartment. I thought in the meantime I'd stay here with you, then we can move into the new place together.'

She studied her fingernails, admiring the pearly glow. 'Is it a penthouse?'

'Is *what* a penthouse?'

'The apartment you're taking.' There was a pause. 'Well, *is* it?'

'I don't know. What the hell does it matter? We'll find a penthouse if that's what you want.'

She smiled at last, pleased and purry. 'Yes, that's what I want. Can I start looking tomorrow? It's going to be too crowded for the two of us here.' She held out her arms to him. 'I'm sorry I've been bitchy but it's been a busy day.'

He fell into her arms and kissed her, feeling the familiar immediate desire rise in him. She kissed him hard, running her tongue across his teeth and scratching the back of his neck with sharp nails. He started to reach for her body, but she pushed him away and leaped up. 'Not now, baby. Let's go to dinner, and then – think of it – we can come back home together. It will be a whole different scene.'

She switched on the stereo, and the sound of the Stones filled the room. She danced around, throwing off her sweater and wriggling out of her slacks in time to the music. She wore a brief white bra and the shiny white boots.

He watched her, mesmerized. 'Don't you ever wear panties?'

'Why spoil the line?' She laughed. 'Does it bother you? I've never had any complaints before!'

She vanished into the bathroom, and he heard the sound of a bath running. He followed her in. She was bending over the bath, filling it with bubbles. She had discarded the bra, but the boots remained.

He grabbed her from behind. She struggled weakly, half laughing. He tried to hold onto her and get out of his clothes at the same time, but she slipped and fell into the bath. By this time she was helpless with laughter, very wet, and covered in bubbles. She stuck her legs over the side of the bath with her boots still on.

He undressed hurriedly and followed her into the bath. The water cascaded over the side.

'I think I'm going to like living here,' he said.

Chapter Thirteen

The sun was streaming into the bedroom and David couldn't sleep any longer. Claudia lay sprawled beside him, taking up more than her share of the bed. She claimed she couldn't sleep with the curtains closed, which accounted for the fact that every morning the light woke him too early. He glanced at his watch. It was only half-past six, and they hadn't got to bed until four. He felt tired and dreadful and hung over. It was no use getting up and pulling the curtains now, as he couldn't go back to sleep once he was awake.

The spacious bedroom was a mess. Claudia had a habit of stepping out of her clothes all over the place and just leaving them. One had to pick one's way through the debris in the mornings.

It's amazing, he thought, how my life has changed in six short months.

The new dress he had bought her lay in a crumpled ball at the bottom of the bed. It was red pleated chiffon. She had seen it in a window in Bond Street, and he had surprised her with it the next day. The surprise had cost him a bomb.

He picked it up. She had spilled a glass of wine on it, and there was a crumpled stain.

In the green-marble bathroom leading off the bedroom, the mess continued. She had not emptied the bath, and it was filled with cold, dirty water. Bottles of makeup and hairbrushes and perfumes were scattered everywhere. The sink was clogged with soap and hair left to congeal beneath a dripping gold tap.

Beneath the mess it was a beautiful apartment. A penthouse, as she had wanted, in a new apartment building in Kensington. It cost far too much money a week. A fortune, in fact. But Claudia loved it and did not care to move.

He emptied the old water and picked up the bath towels. He really wished she would learn to be tidy, but it seemed impossible for her. With Linda, there had never been a thing out of place.

He went through a mirrored hallway to the kitchen. Here there were stale cups of half-drunk coffee, dirty dishes piled high, full ashtrays creating a bad odour.

Fortunately it was Friday, which meant that they had a new cleaning woman starting. The last one had left in disgust when she found out they weren't married, leaving a cryptic note saying, 'I'm not used to such filth.' At first he had thought she was referring to the state Claudia left things in, but the porter had told him what she really meant.

He made a cup of strong tea and managed to burn a couple of pieces of toast. Claudia had acquired a small, yappy Yorkshire terrier, which suddenly came bounding in, anxious for a walk, no doubt. It usually slept on the bed with them and would burrow beneath the covers at night. David hated it. He couldn't stand small dogs.

He left it sniffing around the kitchen and went into the huge, open-plan living-dining room. This was the *pièce de résistance* of the apartment, a beautiful spacious room, one wall completely glass, leading onto a landscaped patio. Another wall marble and the rest of the wall-space mirrored. The room was chaotic. They had had people in for drinks before going out the previous evening, and half-empty glasses seemed to be all over the place. Overflowing ashtrays, spilled nuts, magazines, photographs of Claudia, cushions on the floor. Thank God it would all be cleared up today. David liked order.

He went to the front door and collected his papers, extracting *The Times* and *Guardian* from among the various film and fashion magazines Claudia seemed to have delivered daily.

He drank his tea – it was too strong. Ate his toast – it was burnt. Read the papers through bleary eyes. Soon it would be time to get dressed and go off to work.

* * *

Linda woke early. The sun was shining and it was a lovely day. She felt good. At last she was starting to enjoy the selfish pleasures of sleeping alone. Taking up the whole of the bed, waking and sleeping when she pleased, always being able to get into the bathroom.

It had been hard at first, the decision to get a divorce. She kept thinking of the children without a father. But the fact that David had moved out and set up home with Claudia had helped her to be strong.

She had found a good lawyer and put herself in his hands. It was quite simple, really.

Today was the day she was going to appear in court, stand calmly before a judge, and state the facts. Her lawyer, a short, stocky, grey-haired man, would be by her side. An inquiry agent would be there to offer relevant information. Her counsel was tall, attractive, and sympathetic. They had all assured her it would go quite smoothly. It was undefended and clear-cut.

She dressed, choosing her clothes carefully. A dark-brown neat suit, low-heeled shoes, not too much makeup. Surveying herself in the mirror, she thought she looked the part. An abandoned wife, sad, courageous, alone.

The children were staying with her mother. She ate a solitary breakfast of boiled eggs and coffee, wishing that she hadn't sent them away, wishing that their noisy laughter filled the house.

When she finished in court, she was going by train to join them for the weekend, and they would all return to the house together on Monday.

The house belonged to her now. Financial arrangements had been amicable. She had the house and a fairly generous support settlement for herself and the two children.

David visited the children every weekend, either on Saturday or Sunday. Linda always managed to avoid seeing him. In fact, she hadn't seen him for three months, and then it had been in her lawyer's office to make the financial settlement final.

She made only one stipulation about his seeing the children, and that was that she didn't want them in Claudia's company at all. He didn't argue on that point.

She finished her coffee. Soon it would be time to go to her lawyer's office and accompany him to court.

* * *

Claudia woke at eleven. There was someone ringing the doorbell. She groped her way to the front door, struggling into a flimsy pink negligee covered with makeup stains.

A short, squat woman stood facing her. 'I'm Mrs. Cobb,' she announced. 'The agency sent me.' She had heavy red hands and a scrubbed old face.

'Come in, Mrs. Cobb,' Claudia said, stifling a yawn. 'I'm afraid it's an awful mess, but I'm sure you'll cope.' She took her into the kitchen and gestured under the sink. 'You'll find everything you need there. Excuse me if I leave you to it. I had a very late night.'

Mrs. Cobb looked grimly around and didn't say anything.

Claudia took an open can of peaches from the fridge and tipped them into a dish. 'My breakfast,' she said with a bright smile, and stopping to collect the magazines and papers from the living room, she went into the bedroom.

Propped comfortably back in bed, she leafed idly through the papers, the *Daily Mail* being her favourite. It was the show page that interested her. She scanned it eagerly, looking as usual for any mention of Conrad Lee. She was delighted. Today there was a whole article on the location of his film in Israel. It stated that the company would be returning to England at the end of the week for studio work.

She made a big pencil ring around the piece and phoned her agent on the shell-pink bedside telephone. She still had two days' work to do on Conrad's film. Things had become rather complicated, and the unit had gone on location before reaching her scenes. However, the film company had given her agent constant promises that as soon as they returned she would be needed for her two days' work.

She gave her agent the good news, and he promised to look into it immediately.

She stretched languidly. The past few months since moving to the penthouse had been fun, although David was becoming a bit of a bore. The penthouse was the most beautiful apartment. All her friends were very impressed. She had done lots of photo-sessions there, and she was always pleased when they appeared in various magazines – saying lovely young actress and model, Claudia Parker, relaxing in her luxurious penthouse.

Giles was coming over at two o'clock to do a nude layout for a prominent American men's magazine. She hoped David would be working late as he disliked Giles intensely, in spite of the fact that he didn't even know she had had an affair with him. Anyway, if he knew she was doing a nude layout he would be furious. He was very old fashioned that way.

The magazine was paying her and Giles a lot of money to do the spread. And anyway, she didn't mind showing off her body. After all, it was certainly worth showing.

She lounged back in bed, yawning. Soon it would be time to start preparing herself: until then she could relax.

* * *

David arrived at his office tired and bad-tempered.

His secretary greeted him with a worried face. 'Mr. Cooper, your uncle wants to see you at once. His assistant said you should go straight to his office.'

What now? Being summoned by Uncle Ralph was never good news. His uncle had been most disapproving about his split-up with Linda. Divorce was a frowned-upon sin, and Uncle Ralph could be very religious when it suited him.

Uncle Ralph was sitting like a small, bald buzzard behind his desk in his early-Victorian-style office. His secretary, Penny, a wide-eyed blond, ushered David in.

He appraised her sexy long legs in her ultrashort skirt. Trust Uncle Ralph to have the only good-looking secretary in the building.

'Good morning, David,' Uncle Ralph grunted. 'Sit down – sit down. Wanted to have a word with you about the Fulla Health Beans account.'

'We don't have it anymore.'

'Exactly – exactly. That's what I want to talk to you about.'

His uncle launched into a long lecture about why they had lost the account, which to his way of thinking was because of David's unenthusiastic attitude and the fact that he always seemed tired. He hinted that perhaps the job was too much for him.

David listened carefully, dissecting every word Uncle Ralph said, because every word Uncle Ralph said always meant something else. What he was actually saying was, 'Don't come in here dragging your arse because you've been up with a hot piece all night. Either work or get the hell out.' He concluded the lecture with the information that Mr. Taylor of the Fulla Beans account was in town for one more night, and that he was prepared to reconsider his decision about withdrawing the account.

'Now, you take him out to dinner,' Uncle Ralph said. 'Tell him our plans, lay it on thick. Get him drunk, entertain him. Take him to a nightclub and fix him up with a hostess. Keep him happy. Whatever happens, I want that account back.'

'Yes, sir.' David got up.

Penny was sitting behind her desk in the outer office, legs crossed neatly beneath her desk. She smiled at him, an open invitation in her innocent wide eyes. He wondered vaguely if she was sleeping with the ugly old buzzard; the rumour around the building said she was. He wouldn't mind knocking a piece of that off, get one over on Uncle.

He leaned over her desk. 'How come I only ever see you here?'

Her smile widened and she started to reply, but the buzzer rang on her desk and she jumped up quickly. Uncle Ralph had anticipated the pass and was summoning her to the safety of his office.

She scampered off, sexy legs seductive beneath a short skirt.

David returned morosely to his own office and his own secretary, who was pale and mousy and flat-chested. She had an intense crush on him which she tried to conceal, making it all the more obvious.

'Mr. Cooper,' she said anxiously, 'is everything all right?'

'Everything's fine.' He sat glumly at his desk. The thought of entertaining Mr. Taylor of Fulla Beans to an evening on the town was depressing.

'Oh, dear, Mr. Cooper.' His secretary was almost wringing her hands. 'Oh, dear, it had to happen today too.'

'What's so special about today?'

'It's your divorce today.' She lowered her eyes. 'Well, I mean—'

So it was – he had forgotten all about it. It seemed strange that Linda could go into a court somewhere and divorce him and he didn't even have to be there. It didn't seem right.

His lawyer had written informing him of the date a while ago. He had said that they would send someone along purely as a formality.

His secretary stood nervously by the desk.

'Thanks for the cheerful reminder, Miss Field,' he said.

She flushed. 'I'm so sorry – I thought you knew…' Her words trailed off. 'Would you like some coffee, Mr. Cooper?'

'That would be nice, Miss Field.'

She fled gratefully, almost tearfully, from his office.

'Sonofabitch!' he muttered. *'Sonofabitch!'*

* * *

The entrance hallway into the courts exuded an atmosphere of gloom. There were people scurrying in all directions, and long passages and stairs everywhere. The overall atmosphere was most depressing.

Linda's lawyer gripped her firmly by the arm and manoeuvred her up various flights of stairs and into a series of old elevators. It seemed to take ages to get to wherever they were going.

'I hope your case will be heard before the luncheon recess,' he said. 'Chances are that it will be.'

'How long will it all take?' she asked nervously.

'Not too long. It's all very straightforward. Shouldn't require a lot of time.'

They had arrived in a long hallway with benches along the walls, and this, Linda presumed, was where they would wait. It was crowded with people, and there was a scattering of men in white curled wigs and black gowns.

Her lawyer called one of them over. 'This is your counsel, Mr. Brown.'

Mr. Brown was tall and distinguished-looking, with a tanned, crinkly face. He had a soothing, hypnotic voice, and he discussed the questions he would ask Linda briefly.

She felt sick. The whole thing was so awful. Her stomach was fluttering. She wondered if there was a ladies' room close at hand where she could go and collapse.

Her lawyer said, 'I think it might be a good idea if we go in and sit through a couple of cases before yours. It will give you a chance to see how things are done.'

She nodded bleakly. He led her through an ordinary door into an ordinary room, and she got a jolting shock. Instead of a huge, stately-looking courtroom as she had imagined, it was a small plain room with about six rows of benches where onlookers sat. There was a small, slightly raised desk where the judge presided, and a raised wooden dais where the witness stood. It was awful. Everyone was so close to everyone else. It was like someone's living room converted into a court for a day.

She sat on a hard wooden bench. A slightly built man was standing on the witness dais being questioned. 'And did you know at that time that your wife had had intercourse with Mr. Jackson?'

'Yes, sir.'

'And it was the same day that she packed her bags and left?'

'Yes, sir.'

'Leaving you in the matrimonial home with the children of your marriage, Jennifer and Susan?'

'Yes, sir.'

The case droned on, the slightly built man expressionless as he was asked question after question.

The judge sat wisely on his bench, nodding occasionally and looking for all the world like a senile old owl. At the conclusion of evidence he said, in hardly more than a mumble, 'Divorce granted. Custody of the children. Maintenance referred to chambers. Next case, please.'

The expressionless slight man suddenly broke into smiles, his shoulders straightened, and he left the room happily.

The next case was a mousy-looking blond with a heavy cockney accent who was out to divorce Joe – from the sound of it a wildly attractive sex maniac.

It's so unfair, Linda thought, we're the innocent ones, and we're the ones who have to stand up in this stupid little room and reveal the most personal aspects of our lives.

'Were your marital relationships satisfactory at first?' her counsel asked.

'I should say so!' the mousy blond replied, drawing a muffled, ribald laugh from somewhere in the courtroom.

At last it was Linda's turn. She stood shakily in the witness stand, horribly aware of how close everyone was to her. She resented the rows of spectators. Why *should* they be allowed to sit there and stare and listen? It wasn't fair. After she was sworn in, her counsel began the questions. She answered in a muffled, quiet voice, eyes staring straight ahead.

A document was produced from an inquiry agent, and the judge inspected it briefly. Her counsel continued with the questions, which were really statements of fact which she had only to confirm. Eventually he indicated to the judge that he was finished.

The judge adjusted his glasses, peered for a few brief seconds at Linda, and then said, 'Divorce granted, custody of the two children, and costs to be paid by the husband. Maintenance and access referred to chambers.'

It was all over. She left the stand in a daze. Her lawyer rushed over and took her arm. 'Congratulations,' he whispered.

* * *

Giles was late, of course. He was always late. When he arrived he was laden with cameras and looked tired. 'Give me some strong black coffee, darling,' he said. 'I've had a terrible morning shooting bras in the middle of the New Forest.' He collapsed in a chair, stretching his legs out and yawning. 'Y'know, this is a great pad, almost worth putting up with your boyfriend for.'

'Almost?' questioned Claudia. She had done a skilful makeup. Pale, creamy base, cleverly blended blusher, pale lipstick and huge fluttery eyes. She looked fabulous.

'Yeah, almost. I mean, darling, he's such a pain. Hey, you look great. Wish we were shooting this at night. How late can I stay?'

'Until David gets home. You know how jealous he is. I'll give him a buzz around five and see what time he'll be here.'

'I want to shoot some wild stuff on the terrace – sort of get you silhouetted against the view of London jazz. Lots of hair flowing about and all that shit.'

'Sounds good to me.' She was wearing a pink denim shirt tucked into matching pants with a huge gold-buckled belt and white boots.

'Nice outfit,' he said. 'We can start off with that, discarding it bit by bit.'

'So how's your love life?' she asked. 'Still with that skinny model?'

'Yeah, we break up about every two weeks regularly, but then it's back-together-again time.'

'I see her on the cover of every magazine I pick up. It's amazing, 'cos she's not really that great-looking, but she photographs beautifully.'

'She's got a camera face, y'know. She sees a camera and the face switches on, comes to life. Otherwise, it's just static. I guess our affair keeps going because she's really screwing my camera and I love the results. She's making me a bomb. I can't miss with anything I shoot of her.'

The phone rang. It was Claudia's agent with good news. It was true: the unit was returning in a few days, and she would probably be needed the following week.

'The director is flying in today,' her agent said, 'and the company is going to try and pin him down to a definite date.'

'Fabulous.' She was delighted. She had waited six months for this.

'Let's get started,' Giles said when she hung up, 'before I go to sleep.'

He worked fast, using three different cameras. He threw himself completely into it, becoming utterly absorbed in what he was doing.

Claudia of course blossomed before a camera, pouting, smiling, giving a tiger snarl, big, big sexy eyes always innocently staring, lips open and glossy. She undid the pink shirt, letting it fall casually open. There was nothing underneath.

After a while Giles said, 'Take your shirt off and fold your arms across your boobies. That's it – great! Give me a snarl. That's beautiful, baby. One leg slightly bent – a surprised look, marvellous! Now cover your boobies with your hands, give me the big-eyed-baby look – beautiful!' He kept shooting picture after picture. 'You look terrific. Turn your back to me and swing your head around quickly, let your hair fall – great! Hey, listen, I've got an idea, if you don't mind getting wet. Put the shirt back on and I'll hose you down with water – it'll look dynamite!' He picked up the water hose used to water the plants and turned it on her.

She screamed and laughed. 'It's cold!'

He dropped the hose and picked up his camera.

He was right, it was effective. Her clothes had moulded themselves to her body, and her nipples stood out firm and strong through the shirt.

After an hour on the terrace Giles said, 'Let's go inside, baby. I've got some beautiful stuff of you out here.'

She was shivering.

'Lead the way to the shower,' he said. 'I don't want you catching cold. Strip off slowly. I want to capture it all.'

He followed her into the bathroom with his cameras, catching every moment as she wriggled out of her wet clothes and secured her hair with a couple of pins. Next she stood under the shower, her body gleaming as the rivulets of water hit her.

He said, 'Lean back, close your eyes, just let the water fall over you. Great! Bring your arms up behind your head. Lovely, darling, that's lovely.'

They finished in the bathroom and Giles said, 'Now for some stuff in the bedroom, and then we should have it made.'

She put on a filmy black chiffon robe trimmed with feathers and let her hair down. The robe was transparent, casting a black haze over her body.

'Lie right in the middle of the bed, bring your head up, bend one knee ever so slightly, no, your left knee, darling – that's it. Wet your lips and give me the look. No, that's too hard, a soft look like you just made it.' He took a few shots and then put his camera down. 'Listen, you want these pictures to look really good?'

'Of course I do – what's the matter?' She sat up, her perfect breasts falling free of the robe.

'You just haven't got the right look, you're trying too hard. You gotta relax, kid.'

She stretched. 'I'm relaxed.'

'Yeah. I know, but you know what I want – I want the cat-that-just-got-the-cream look.'

'So give me the cream…' She reached for him.

'Just what I had in mind.'

They made love easily, slowly, almost offhandedly, and afterward he got quickly up and picked up his camera. 'Stay just as you are. That's perfect. *Now* you look authentic!'

* * *

David phoned Claudia at five o'clock. He had been trying to make up his mind whether to take her along with Mr. Taylor of Fulla Beans or not. Eventually he had decided it would be better not to, as he would pay more attention to her than to Mr. Taylor, and that would defeat the purpose of the whole outing.

'What are you doing?' he asked.

She giggled. 'Just lying around.'

He told her about the evening ahead and she said, 'That's all right, I'll find something to do.'

'Why don't you get an early night? I'll wake you when I get in.'

She suddenly laughed. 'Hey, David, I feel like a wife. Are you sure you haven't got some hot little number standing by your side?'

'Honestly, Claudia, don't be so stupid.'

She laughed. 'Don't worry about it, I wouldn't mind. Anything *you*can do, I can do too.'

'It's a business dinner. Now, what *are* you going to do?'

She paused, then said, 'The President of America.'

'What?'

She laughed again. 'I'm only joking. Go on, I believe you. Have a nice dinner. I shall probably ask a few people over, and we'll sit around and wait for your esteemed return.'

'All right,' he said reluctantly. 'An early night would do you much more good.'

'You're beginning to sound so uptight.' She mimicked his voice. 'An early night would do you much more good!'

He ignored her comment. 'I'll phone you later. Be good.'

'Yes, sir. Anything else, sir?'

'Good-bye.' He put the phone down, annoyed at the way she spoke to him. Annoyed by the fact that he was still so jealous of her. Annoyed by the fact she was going to ask people over. He would have to try and find Mr. Taylor a randy hostess and get rid of him early. He went into his private bathroom to change his shirt and shave.

Miss Field knocked nervously to say good night, and he rewarded her with a glimpse of his naked chest. She blushed deeply, and he wondered idly if she had ever been laid. He really couldn't imagine it. She wore long, knee-length pink bloomers which he had noticed when she sat opposite him taking dictation. Also she was flat-chested, and who would want to lay a flat-chested, ugly girl? Once he had screwed the most horrifying-looking girl, cross-eyed, bad teeth, acne, but she had had the best and biggest knockers he'd ever seen and wild legs. She had been a great lay, too, but he hadn't bothered to see her again. That face was too much.

David had met Mr. Taylor once before, briefly. He was fat and middle-aged with thinning brown hair plastered neatly to his scalp to give the impression that it wasn't thinning at all, but just grew that way. He had a thick Lancashire accent and a thick Lancashire wife with two matching sons. He was a bore.

David met him in the bar of his hotel. He had been drinking lager beer but switched to Scotch as soon as David arrived. David tried to be charming – but Burt Taylor's idea of charming was a person who drank fast and told an everlasting run of dirty stories.

David tried to please, and Burt rewarded him with hearty guffaws and conspiratorial winks. By the time they arrived at the restaurant, David was well on the way and Burt already there – drunk, that is.

David tried to insert a little business into the conversation, but Burt switched it neatly back to the subject of sex by remarking how he bet David had a lot of hot ones passing through his job.

'All those little model girls,' Burt said, 'that's how they get the job, by sleeping with you, isn't it?' David didn't argue.

Eventually they left the restaurant with Burt singing snatches of old rugby songs.

David patted him on the back. 'Let's go and have some fun.'

They went to a plush nightclub filled with tired, painted hostesses and jocular, lecherous, out-of-town businessmen on expense accounts. The maitre d', a smooth, suave Cypriot, asked if they would care to meet two nice young ladies.

'Yes,' Burt boomed. 'Only make sure they're not all that nice.' He roared with laughter.

A few minutes later two girls arrived at their table. One was tall and buxom, with red hair and a strapless green velvet dress; she was about thirty. The other was smaller and slightly timid-looking – in spite of a dress cut low enough to reveal almost all of her scrawny bosom. She was very young.

They both tried to attach themselves to David, but he excused himself from the table, realizing he hadn't phoned Claudia.

A man answered the phone, and he was told to hang on while the mystery voice located Claudia. 'Shit!' David mumbled. There was so much noise and music coming through the receiver. What was going on? He hung on grimly, feeling the alcohol pounded out of his body by a sudden mad anger. By the time Claudia spoke he felt almost sober.

'Hi, darling,' she cooed. 'Where are you? I'm having a marvellous time. It turned into a party.'

'Who answered the phone? Who's there?'

'I don't know, heaps of people. Hurry home, baby.' And she hung up.

He stood in the booth for a few minutes, then, intent on getting rid of Burt Taylor, he hurried back to the table.

Burt had ordered champagne, naturally, since David would be paying the check. The two hostesses were flanking him on either side, and he looked blissfully happy.

David thought the best thing to do was to get hold of the big brassy redhead and proposition her to take Mr. Burt Taylor off somewhere. He obviously preferred her to the younger one.

There was a corny Latin-American band playing. 'How about a dance?' he said to the redhead.

She smelled heavily of cheap perfume and pressed herself groin to groin with him. 'I like you,' she lisped.

He managed to push her away a little. 'Hey, listen, you want to make yourself some money?'

She looked interested while he explained the proposition. They bargained, reached an agreement, and sat down, David carefully slipping her the money beforehand.

Burt Taylor seemed put out. He took David to one side.

'I saw her first, boyo. I don't want the skinny bit.'

David smiled. This was going to be easy. 'It's all right, she can't stop talking about you. You've got it made.'

'In that case...' Burt leered, 'we won't be wasting much more time here.'

David reckoned another half an hour and he would be home. He patted Burt on the shoulder. 'I'll get the check,' he said.

* * *

There were photographers outside the court waiting for Linda. The fact that Claudia Parker had been named as the other woman made the case newsworthy.

'Over here,' one of them called.

Linda rushed straight ahead, her lawyer gripping her arm. The cameras clicked.

'What do they want?' she questioned. 'Can't they leave people alone? I'm nobody.'

Her lawyer hailed a passing taxi and pushed her in. 'It's best for you to get away from here. Congratulations again. We'll be in touch with you.'

'Don't you want a lift?' she said, trying to delay being left on her own.

'No. My office is just around the corner. Thank you all the same. Good-bye, Mrs. Cooper.' He was gone, and the taxi was moving off down the street.

'Where to, lady?' asked the cab driver.

She sat there in a daze. It had all happened so quickly, it was like a dream.

'Where to, lady?' the cab driver repeated impatiently.

She didn't feel like rushing straight to the station. She felt like a drink and a cigarette and a half-hour of quiet relaxation. 'The Dorchester,' she said. It was the first place that came to mind.

The bar was fairly crowded, mostly with businessmen, but she found a secluded table, ordered a sherry, and sat back to enjoy it. She decided she would have lunch there. It was good to be on her own. She would order smoked salmon, fresh strawberries with cream, maybe even drink champagne.

'It is Linda Cooper, isn't it?'

She looked up, hesitated, and then said, 'Jay – Jay Grossman. Why, I would hardly have recognized you. What a wonderful tan.'

He sat down, smiling. 'I just got in from Israel. How are you? It's been months and months.'

'I'm fine.' She smiled back at him.

'And David?'

'David? I don't really know. I just divorced him about half an hour ago.'

Jay looked surprised. 'You really did it, then. Was it about that night?'

She nodded. 'Yes, it was about that night. He's living with her now.'

'Wow, you certainly mean what you say.'

'How is Lori?'

'Lori is very happy. Lori is married to a Texas oil tycoon who buys her two mink coats a week, so she's very happy.'

'You mean you've divorced too?'

'Yes, I'm divorced yet again. We do these things quickly in the States. She went to Nevada and shed me in six weeks. Extreme mental cruelty, I think she said. Then she married this other man the very next day. The only good thing is she didn't knock me for any alimony or settlements, so I was lucky. Supporting the other two exes costs me enough.' He laughed. 'Are you meeting anyone?'

She shook her head.

'What about having lunch with me?'

She smiled. She liked Jay. 'I'd love to.'

'Good.' He stood up. 'I've just got to rearrange a few things. I'll be right back.'

After he left, Linda quickly took out her compact. She studied her face and added more lipstick. She wished she looked a bit more glamorous, but she had deliberately dressed down to appear in court. Jay was a very attractive man. Since separating from David, Linda had only been out on one date, partly because her lawyer had warned her not to, and partly because she didn't want to. The episode with Paul had left its mark, and she preferred to stay at home or visit married friends. The one evening she had gone out had been a bore. And to add insult to injury, her date had expected her to go to bed with him. Divorcees, she gathered from him, were supposed to include sex in the evening's activities.

Jay returned to the table. 'Everything's under control. Where would you like to eat?'

They decided to stay where they were. They moved into the restaurant, and Jay entertained her with amusing anecdotes about the location and idle gossip about the people involved. He took her hand over coffee and said, 'My God, it's nice to be with someone who has a brain and not just a body. You know, I really like you. Linda, you're a nice person.'

She smiled a little stiffly. She didn't want Jay to think of her as such a nice person. Nice was such a dull word, it conjured up twinsets and sensible shoes.

He looked at his watch. 'Wow – it's nearly three o'clock. I've got to rush.' He called for the check. 'Let me drop you at the station. I've got a studio car.'

'No, it's out of your way. I can easily get a cab.'

'If you insist. I'll put you in the cab, though.'

They left the restaurant and walked through the lobby, where Jay was hailed by a couple standing there. The woman was tall, blond, and pretty. The man short, stocky, and red-faced.

The man said, 'Oh, Mr. Grossman, sorry you couldn't make lunch. This is my client, Miss Susan Standish.'

Miss Susan Standish smiled a direct smile at Jay. She had very small white teeth and looked even prettier when smiling.

Jay smiled back. Linda saw his eyes flicker with interest as they swept over Miss Susan Standish. Tall, pretty blondes were obviously his type.

'I'll be right back,' he said, and took Linda to the entrance.

He made no comment about the couple he had obviously stood up for lunch. He kissed her on the cheek. 'Linda, let's do this again sometime. When will you be back?'

'Thank you for a lovely lunch, Jay. I'll be home on Monday.'

He saw her into a cab. 'I'll talk to you then,' he said.

* * *

The phone rang and Claudia stretched languorously across the bed and picked it up. She spoke briefly, and with a grin she hung up.

'Baby,' she said to Giles, 'tonight we can have good times. David won't be home till late!'

Giles said, 'What are we waiting for? Let's have a party. Get on the phone. Call the liquor store first.'

They picked out names at random. Giles would say, 'Remember that kooky little girl who always wore those terrible thigh-length black boots…' and they tracked her down, inviting another half-dozen people en route. Claudia changed into a startling silver-lamé cat suit. Giles snatched a nap, sprawled across her bed, and eventually people began to appear.

By the time David phoned again the party was in full swing. Claudia was completely stoned. She didn't even know who half the people were. The music was so loud that the tenants in the apartment below had complained three times. They had stopped phoning, as the last time a beautifully spoken debutante had told them exactly what to do in explicit detail. She was now accommodating an out-of-work window cleaner on the couch in full view of everyone.

'Great party!' Giles said. 'What happens when big daddy comes walking in?'

'Big daddy's going to have to join in the fun, or big daddy can walk right on out again.'

'Darling, sweetie pie – how divine of you to invite me.'

Claudia blinked, focusing slowly. 'Shirley, baby, how are you?'

'I'm fine, simply fine. Just got back from the most divine holiday.'

'You look wonderful, all that crazy suntan. Where's the Honourable whatnot?'

'Ditched him, darling. I've got the most divine man now, simply a poppet. You'll be amazed.'

'Grab a drink and join in the fun. It's all happening here…' She trailed off as an Italian waiter type grabbed her from behind. 'You is beautiful,' he said. 'I eat you up.'

'Really,' Shirley said, 'it looks like you're in good hands. I'll see you later, sweetie.' She left Claudia struggling with the Italian.

Claudia had never seen him before. 'Leave me alone, you oaf,' she said.

He was very strong. 'You beautiful,' he said proudly. Obviously his English vocabulary was limited. He twisted her around in his arms and kissed her.

'Your breath stinks!' she exclaimed, still struggling.

He held her even tighter and kissed her again.

It was at this moment that David appeared. He stood furiously in the doorway of the apartment, spotted Claudia immediately, and, striding across the room, he hauled the Italian away from her – smashing his fist into his face.

The man slumped to the floor, blood seeping from his nose.

David then turned his attention to Claudia. 'You fucking tramp,' he said, and brought his arm back-handedly across her face.

Nobody really noticed what was going on. The music was too loud and they were all too stoned.

'Get these dregs out of here,' David snarled.

She rubbed her cheek, her eyes huge and filled with tears – more from pain than from anything else. 'You *sonofabitch,'* she screamed. 'How dare you hit me – *how dare you?'*

'I'll do what I want to you. I bought you, didn't I? Now get this damned place clear.'

'You can go to hell and back, you bastard.' She bent to the Italian and cradled his head in her arms.

'I'm warning you, Claudia, you're pushing me too far.'

She ignored him.

He stood for a few seconds, then said, 'Right.' He marched into the bedroom.

It was at this particular moment that Giles was reaching a hard-fought-for climax with a skinny redhead. It was unfortunate that it happened to be right in the middle of David's bed.

David swore loudly, but nothing bothered Giles. He kept on going, although the girl squeaked and attempted to object.

David grimly took a suitcase from the top of a cupboard. He methodically sorted his clothes from Claudia's, packing as much as he could.

Giles and the girl got up. She glared at David as she rearranged her clothes. 'Some people just don't care,' she muttered. 'They barge in anywhere.'

Giles made a mock bow. 'Performance over, next show at four o'clock.'

They walked out of the bedroom.

David locked the door behind them and continued packing. He finally filled three suitcases. His mind was cold with anger.

He unlocked the bedroom and strode to the front door with two of the cases. The party was still in full swing. He returned for the third suitcase.

'Bye-bye, darling,' Claudia yelled above the noise. She reeled across the room toward him. The front zipper on her cat suit was undone to her waist, and her breasts pushed forward to escape. Her hair was wild, and blood smeared her face.

'You look lovely,' he said. 'Just like the drunken little slut you are.'

She laughed. 'Get stuffed,' she shouted. 'Get lost, asshole – don't come back. You're a bloody bore.'

Giles joined her. 'You tell him, kid,' he said, slipping his hand inside her open zipper.

She made an obscene gesture and turned her back.

David left.

Chapter Fourteen

'Well, look, darling, what *is* happening?' Claudia's voice was edgy and cold on the phone. 'I mean, they've been back ten days now, and they should be able to tell us *something?*'

Her agent was noncommittal. 'I can't get any definite date out of them.'

'But I signed a contract for two days' work – a contract, remember?'

'Yes, I know. But they've paid you for the work you were supposed to do. They don't have to use you.'

She snorted angrily. 'What kind of an agent *are* you? I'm supposed to be in that film. It's a big film, and it will do me a lot of good – a lot more good than these walk-on bits you keep offering me. If you can't do it, tell me, and I'll get someone who can!'

Her agent's voice was resigned. 'I'm doing my best.'

'Your best's not good enough. Forget it, I'll do it myself. *I'll* call Conrad Lee.' She slammed the phone down.

The apartment was in a terrible mess. The new cleaner had walked out the day after the party. Actually, the party had still been going on the next morning when she arrived, and she had taken one horrified look at the red-headed boy wearing Claudia's cat suit who answered the front door and left.

It had been a good party, lasted three days in all. Claudia didn't remember much about it, really – but Giles assured her it had been a mind blower.

David hadn't returned. He hadn't phoned and he hadn't communicated in any way, although a mousy secretary had arrived one day about a week later to collect his mail and request that in future it be forwarded to his office.

Claudia didn't miss him. She was rather glad he had gone. Life was too confining with someone watching every move you made. She had fallen in with David because it was easy, and he had left his wife, and it just sort of happened. It was rather nice having all the bills paid and lots of new clothes and no problems.

Now she would have to think about going back to work, a secret job she had which had always given her enough money to lead a comfortable, independent life. It would be better to be in Conrad's movie and become a star and make lots more money that way.

The other way gave her a vicarious thrill, though, and none of her friends – no one – knew about it. She had always kept it a closely guarded secret. Before she was living with David all her friends had wondered but never found out how she managed to be so financially secure and independent. The job excited her. She wore wigs and did special creative makeup jobs, completely disguising her own features. She starred in glorious Technicolor in porno movies! In four years she had been in thirty of them, making a lot of money along the way. So successful was she at the disguise jobs that she was known as three completely different girls, all in constant demand by the voyeurs who got to see the finished products. If she wanted to work again, all it would take was a phone call. This is Evette – or Carmen – or Maria – and arrangements would be made. She was paid cash, and she contacted *them* – they had no way of reaching her. It was a satisfactory arrangement.

However, she wasn't sure that she wanted to go back to doing that. Sometimes her co-stars left a lot to be desired, and of course, if you weren't in the right mood, it could be pretty grim.

No – to appear in Conrad's movie was the best thing, and if her agent couldn't fix it, she certainly could. Conrad would probably be delighted to hear from her again.

She phoned the hotel he had stayed at on his previous visit, but he wasn't registered there. She phoned the studio and spoke to a secretary who took her name and said she would pass Mr. Lee her message. She tried to find out where he was living, but the girl was polite but firm – 'We're not allowed to disclose Mr. Lee's address,' she said. 'I'll certainly see he gets your message.' It wasn't very satisfactory. Claudia wanted to get to him personally.

Giles would be able to find out. Giles was able to get hold of anyone. She called him at his studio, but there was no reply.

'Dammit!' she muttered, finally getting up.

There was a stack of bills by the front door. David had stopped paying for everything since he had left, and the bills were steadily mounting. She couldn't stick him with any of them, as the apartment and everything was in her name. It was a question of getting hold of Conrad and becoming a star.

Linda stayed in the country with her parents and the children much longer than she expected to. It was so peaceful. The children were out playing all day while she sat in the house with her mother fussing around her. It was very relaxing, and knowing that to return to London was to be the beginning of a new life, she clung onto the limbo period of being with her parents.

Her mother wanted her to stay there permanently. 'Sell your house,' she urged. 'There's plenty of room for you here.'

Linda rejected the offer. Her parents' home was just a temporary retreat, and tempting as the thought was, it would be a mistake to stay. She would be buried there, stifled. Her mother would take care of everything, even to bringing up the children. Linda would become the elder daughter of the family.

One Saturday afternoon David turned up. It was the first time she had seen him since the divorce.

'I tried phoning the house. I was worried,' he said. 'I thought you'd be here.'

Her voice was stilted, cold. 'Why didn't you phone first? Why did you just come?'

He was ill at ease. It was strange to see David groping for words – he who was usually so sure of himself.

'I wanted to see the children.' A note of indignation crept into his voice. 'I'm supposed to see the children, you know.' He looked thin and tired. 'I've left Claudia,' he blurted out.

She looked at him dispassionately. 'Really.'

'You look marvellous,' he said.

She did look well. Her skin was glowing from long walks in the country, and her hair was shining and unset, tied casually back with a ribbon. She looked slim in a pair of slacks and a loose shirt.

She gestured outside. 'The children are in the garden. I'll call them in.'

He put a hand on her arm. 'I said I've left Claudia.'

She brushed his hand impatiently away. 'I heard you the first time, David. I'll get the children.' She walked quickly from the room.

He stayed the whole afternoon, chatting amicably to her parents, entertaining Jane and Stephen with all sorts of games.

David is turning on his well-known charm, Linda thought miserably. I wish he'd go away.

He finally left at six.

Her mother wanted to ask him to stay for dinner, but Linda hissed at her, 'Don't you dare.' His charm had worked. 'He really wants you back,' her mother said after he had gone.

She was really saying you should go back to him. Linda knew the signs.

Her father was less direct. 'That boy needs a father,' he said, when Stephen played up before going to bed.

Her mother said later in the evening, 'Poor David looks so unhappy.'

It was too much for Linda. They just didn't understand. They meant well, but she had had enough.

The next morning she told them she was going back to London, and on Monday morning she packed. Amidst tears from her mother and gruff words of wisdom from her father, she and the children were put safely on a train.

She was glad to be back in her own house. The children were pleased and excited to be reunited with all their books and toys, and cries of 'super' and 'that's mine' rang through the house.

Ana gave her a list of phone messages, and among them were two calls from Jay Grossman. He had left his number. She didn't call back. She thought about it, but somehow she felt if he really wanted to see her, he would try again.

Monica had phoned. They hadn't spoken since the separation; they were David's friends. She phoned her.

Monica was delighted. 'Darling,' she exclaimed, 'I'm having a little dinner party – I'd love you to come.'

Linda was hesitant. 'When?'

'Tomorrow night. I must see you. It's been such ages. Will you come?'

She hesitated. 'I don't know. Have you invited David?'

'What do you take me for? Of course not. I don't want any other excuses. I'll see you tomorrow, eight o'clock. Don't be late.'

It was settled. It might be fun. Monica always invited interesting people. She would go to the hairdresser's and then buy a new dress. It was about time she started going out again.

* * *

Claudia sprawled untidily on a sofa at the back of Giles's studio. He was hard at work photographing a languid brunette clad only in a silver body stocking.

Claudia yawned. 'Why the hell don't you answer your bloody phone? You could have saved me a trip.'

Giles didn't look around; his concentration was completely on the model. After a few minutes he stopped, told the girl to take a break and wandered over to Claudia. He lit a cigarette and stuck it in her mouth.

She took a long drag, spluttered, and choked. 'Jesus Christ! Smoking pot at this time of the day! You're too much!'

He laughed, took it back, and said, 'What do *you* want?'

'I came to see you,' she replied coyly. ''Cos I love you.'

'Cut the crap. I'm busy. What do you want?'

'Actually…' She stretched. 'I need Conrad Lee's number – I thought you could get it for me.'

'Things must be tough if you're chasing him again.'

Her voice was irritable; sometimes she couldn't stand him. 'Things are not tough – and I'm not chasing anyone.'

He laughed. 'Don't forget it's me you're talking to, baby.'

'How could I possibly forget?'

They exchanged stares. 'All right,' he said, 'keep cool. I'll get it for you.' He made a few calls and got her the number.

She wrote it down and smiled. 'Thank you, darling,' she purred.

'That's all right, sweetheart – now get the hell out of here. I've got work to do.'

Claudia went shopping. She bought a white-and-gold silk jersey dress and gold spiky-heeled shoes, unfashionable but sexy. She went to the hairdresser's and had her hair elaborately piled on top of her head.

Back home, she bathed, splashing half a bottle of musky oil into the water. She took two hours with her makeup – worrying until it was perfect.

By the time she was dressed it was seven o'clock. She dialled the number Giles had given her. Conrad's unmistakably accented voice answered.

She smiled. It was all going to work perfectly. She sounded cool and efficient. 'Mr. Lee?'

'Yes.' His voice was gruff.

'I am calling for *Star* magazine. You may know we are featuring your photograph on our cover this week, and I wondered if you might answer a few short questions about yourself.'

He became friendly. 'My picture, huh? Sure, I'll answer a few questions.'

Conceited pig! 'Thank you so much. Mr. Lee, if you will just give me your address, I'll be right over. It will only take a short while.'

He was surprised. 'Can't I answer them now?'

'No, Mr. Lee, it's important to get your comments in person. I'm such a fan!'

'All right, all right.' He gave her his address.

Controlling her laughter she hung up, admired her reflection in the mirror and buzzed the doorman for a cab.

Conrad lived in an imposing house in Belgravia. The door was opened by a manservant in a white jacket who ushered her into the library. She waited patiently for fifteen minutes until at last Conrad lumbered in. He hadn't changed. A fat cigar was stuck between his fleshy lips, and he wore the same green silk smoking jacket.

She arose, deliberately posing her body so that the thin silk dress clung even tighter. She knew she had never looked better. 'Hi.' She smiled provocatively.

He came to an abrupt standstill. She could see he didn't recognize her. He plucked the cigar from his mouth. 'Are you the broad from *Star*?'

'Do I *look* like a lady journalist?'

His piercing eyes roved over her body. His memory stirred. 'Hey – you're the broad from the party I gave.' His voice changed. 'Hey – what's going on here – what is this?'

'You're a difficult man to get hold of. I've left lots of messages for you.'

'So?'

'I thought it was about time we got together again. Don't tell me you've forgotten all the fun we had last time.'

Interest flickered briefly in his eyes. 'Listen, I've got guests. You stay here, and I'll see what I can do.'

He left the room and she smiled triumphantly. It was amazing what a fabulous body could do.

He was gone for a long time. The manservant came in with a drink and left her some magazines. She leafed idly through them, waiting, because eventually he would be back, and then tomorrow morning, enter Claudia Star!

Chapter Fifteen

From the day he walked out on Claudia, David felt depressed. It wasn't that he had wanted to stay, the situation was impossible.

Claudia had turned out to be an out-and-out slut. She lolled around reading magazines all day, only bothering with her appearance if they were going out. She stayed in bed until noon, never tidying the apartment. The only thing she seemed capable of was incessant lovemaking, and whereas before he had lived with her, he had always been ready, now he just couldn't do it. She was insatiable and demanding, never getting enough. David had always prided himself on his sexual appetite, but this was ridiculous.

He was pleased to have an excuse to get out. But depression followed, because instead of dismissing the whole mess from his mind and going home to his wife and children, he was an outcast with nowhere to go except the coldness of a hotel room. No home comforts, just four impersonal walls, an empty bed, and a Do Not Disturb sign.

He returned to work with a vengeance and brooded on the possibilities of getting back together with Linda. He reasoned that she *should* take him back. After all, there were the children to consider. *They* wanted him back. Everything could be like it was before, only this time he wouldn't be such a fool and get hooked up with a tramp like Claudia. He would be more careful, pick and choose, short casual affairs, nothing that Linda could discover.

He phoned his ex-home and the maid informed him that Linda and the children were in the country with her parents. He was pleased. Give her more time to get over it. She was a sensible woman. She would know it was right for them to be together.

The first Saturday he was free he drove down to see her.

She looked surprisingly fresh and well, although her attitude was cold toward him. It was only to be expected.

He told her about leaving Claudia. Her reaction was strangely negative.

Give her time, he thought, she'll come around.

He was charming to her parents. He knew they were back on his side.

Later he drove back to London and called an old girlfriend. She was giggly and a bit stupid but had a great body.

They went to a movie and then back to her place. She was lousy in bed. She had none of the franticness of Claudia or the calmness of Linda. He left after an hour.

On Sunday he woke early with nothing to do. An impulse took him to his office. He had a backlog of letters and other work he never found time for during the week.

He really needed his secretary to be around. Poor, plain Miss Field. Maybe she was available. She looked the sort of person who never made any plans. He phoned her.

Her voice was timid. 'Hello.'

'Miss Field. Mr. Cooper here.'

'Oh!' Her voice became a startled squeak, as if she had been caught doing something she shouldn't have been.

'Miss Field, how do you feel about working today?'

'Oh, Mr. Cooper – oh, really?'

'It's all right if you can't manage it.'

'Oh, no – Oh, Mr. Cooper, of course I can.'

'Good. Get here as fast as you can.'

She was there within the hour, pale and nervous.

'You look very nice today, Miss Field,' he said politely.

She had brushed her thin stringy brown hair down instead of pulling it back, and she wore a harsh scarlet lipstick on her thin, usually colourless mouth. Sunday clothes consisted of a brown dress and blue woollen cardigan. She was a picture of plainness.

They worked efficiently through the day nonstop until the light began to fade, and David suddenly realized it was getting late.

'I suppose we'd better quit,' he said, yawning. 'You must be hungry.'

'Mr. Cooper…' Her voice was hesitant, nervous. 'Perhaps you would care to have a little dinner with me.' A bright red flush was spreading up into her hairline. 'I make it my business to always prepare a *cordon-bleu* dinner on Sundays – one of my little hobbies, and I would be only too delighted if you would sample it.' She added quickly, 'Boeuf Stroganoff, with fresh green salad, followed by lemon meringue pie.'

It sounded good. Besides, he had nowhere else to go. She kept blushing, and he felt sorry for her. 'What a good idea, Miss Field. I'd be glad to.'

She lived in a tiny one-room apartment. The couch, neatly festooned with crochet cushions, obviously did double duty as the bed.

She produced a half-bottle of sherry – too sweet – and he sat and watched television while she pottered about in the kitchen.

She prepared a delicious dinner with which they drank cheap Spanish wine. 'I brought it back from my holiday last year,' she said proudly.

After dinner she was obviously a little tipsy. 'I don't usually drink,' she said with a giggle.

He was also slightly drunk, having consumed half the bottle of wine and most of the sherry before dinner. His attention was riveted to the television screen. The Beauty Maid commercial was on, and there was Claudia in her bath. Familiar sharp pull in his groin.

'Oh, Mr. Cooper, our commercial.' Miss Field sat quickly down beside him on the couch.

He felt the nearness of a leg beside him and rested his hand on her thigh. She shrieked, and before he knew it, her arms were around his neck and she was pulling his mouth toward the thin red line. They kissed, and as Claudia vanished from the screen so his desire vanished with her. But it was too late. Miss Field was already in action. All in the space of seconds, she leaped up, turned the light off, wriggled out of her cardigan, and was back beside him. 'My dearest, I am yours,' she said. 'I have waited for this moment too long.'

He couldn't believe it. The whole thing was ludicrous.

She lay back expectantly, quivering.

What should he do? She was a good secretary. He didn't want to lose her. He didn't want to hurt her feelings.

She was getting impatient. 'David, my dearest, come to me. I am not afraid.'

He took a deep breath and ran his hands tentatively across her bosom. There was no bosom!

Coyly she said, 'I know I am not well endowed, but there is fire in my loins.'

Oh, my God! he thought. What am I getting into?

Tired of waiting, she locked her hands behind his head and pulled his mouth down on hers.

This is a bloody nightmare, he thought. But as her tongue worked on his mouth so his body started to respond, and soon he was ready.

She was angular, bony, and surprisingly strong. She managed to get his pants and shorts off and then her mouth was travelling down his body and she was kissing him, and suddenly it was all over for him in a huge, shaking, furious bout of passion. He screamed, but she didn't stop, sending him into a frenzy. A shudder enveloped her and at last she was still.

They lay in silence – his body sprawled across her at an angle. He could hardly believe what had just taken place. Placid, timid Miss Field Mouse certainly knew what she was doing.

He went and locked himself in the bathroom. His body was covered in red weals where her fingers had dug into him. She was a hot bitch!

When he returned to the room, her cardigan was back on, and she was primly clearing the dishes. She avoided looking at him as he stepped into his shorts and pants.

'Would you like coffee before you go, Mr. Cooper?' she said. Her voice was controlled, only a slight flush across her cheeks indicating what had just taken place.

'Er, no, thank you, Miss Field.' He took his cue from her. 'I really must be on my way.'

'I do hope we can do this again,' she said evenly.

'Yes.' He hesitated. 'Well, good-bye, then. See you at the office tomorrow.'

'Good-bye, Mr. Cooper. See you tomorrow.'

Out in the street he heaved a big sigh. He would have to get rid of her. To have her working with him at the office every day would be a horrible reminder. Next time he would get a pretty secretary – just on the chance he should ever be thrown into an experience like this again.

He thought about Linda with wry longing. He was ready to go home.

* * *

'Linda, darling! You look positively stunning! So slim, so young! This divorce business certainly agrees with you.' Monica led Linda into the living room. 'It's an interesting crowd tonight. No married couples – Jack and I decided it would be more fun. Now let me introduce you.'

There were perhaps twelve people sitting and standing around. Linda recognized Monica's brother, a dress designer. He was with a short, squat woman wearing a very unsuitable silk pajama suit.

'That's Princess Lorenz Alvaro with Rodney,' whispered Monica. 'Exciting, isn't it?'

Linda had never heard of Princess Alvaro, and she didn't see what was so exciting about it, as Rodney was gay.

She was soon chatting quietly to a doctor. A tall and pleasant man. Before they had finished one martini he had invited her to dinner the following evening, and she thought, why not? So she accepted. He was fairly attractive and seemed most taken with her. Definitely a nice man, not a David type at all.

More people arrived, and Linda found herself wedged in a corner, while the doctor told her a long involved story about a patient of his with yellow jaundice. It was rather boring. She smiled politely and wished she hadn't accepted his dinner invitation. Doctor or not, he had a severe case of bad breath.

Idly she glanced around the room. Then she saw Jay and she straightened up, smoothed down her dress, and touched her hair. He hadn't seen her. He was talking to Rodney and Princess Alvaro, and then he was joined by the blond girl who had been in the lobby of the Dorchester the day they had lunched. The blond looked even prettier now in a crisp white pant suit, her hair tied on top of her head with a white ribbon. Jay put his arm around her, and she smiled up at him.

Linda looked away. The doctor droned on.

Monica announced that a cold buffet was being served in the other room.

'I *am* hungry,' Linda said pointedly.

'Good heavens,' said the doctor, 'I must have been boring you stiff. Let's go and eat.' He took her possessively by the elbow and steered her into the other room, where she bumped straight into Jay.

He balanced two plates of food which almost fell. 'Linda!' He sounded pleased.

'Jay,' she said, affecting the same tone.

'Where have you been?'

'In the country with the children.'

'You look terrific.'

Did I look so terrible before? she wondered. 'Thank you.' She couldn't help grinning stupidly.

They stood and smiled at each other, and then the doctor's grip tightened and he said, 'We'd better get our food.'

'Oh, yes.' Linda's heart was beating fast.

'See you in a minute,' Jay said. He winked and imitated an English accent. 'We'd better get our food!'

When Jay was out of hearing distance, the doctor said, 'These American film types are all the same.'

'Oh?'

'You know – brash, vulgar, full of themselves.'

'Do you know Jay Grossman?' Linda asked crossly.

'Let's say we have a mutual friend.'

'Who?' she asked rudely.

'Name no names, hear no pack drill.'

'What?' Suddenly she hated the doctor.

He smiled secretly. 'As a matter of fact, it's one of his ex-wives.'

'Oh.' She tried to sound disinterested.

'A lovely woman,' the doctor continued. 'I believe she had a terrible time with him. She just remarried.'

'Lori?' Linda asked coldly.

The doctor looked surprised. 'Yes. Lori is in London with her husband. He's extremely wealthy.'

166

'How interesting,' she said sarcastically, and quickly helped herself to food before rushing back into the other room. The doctor followed her closely.

There was nowhere to sit.

Jay was with the blond on a sofa. 'Linda,' he called. 'Sit here.'

'Excuse me,' she said to the doctor.

Jay stood up and she sat down. The blond glanced at her, annoyed.

'Susan,' Jay said, 'I want you to meet a very good friend of mine, Linda Cooper.'

'Hello.' Susan's smile was limp.

The doctor squatted on his haunches in front of them, eating from his crowded plate hungrily. Jay drifted away to the other side of the room.

Susan suddenly got up and said to Linda, 'Perhaps your friend would like to sit down.' She moved across the room to join Jay, and the doctor quickly sat beside Linda. She was well and truly stuck as he obviously had no intention of leaving her side.

'Can I drive you home later?' he asked.

'I'm sorry. I have my car with me.'

'Pity.' He shook his head. 'Maybe I should follow to see you get home safely.' He chuckled.

She could have screamed, he was such a bore! She didn't even bother to reply, just jumped up. He got up too.

'Excuse me,' she said firmly, 'I have to go to the ladies' room.'

It was quiet upstairs in Monica's bedroom. She sat at the dressing table and rearranged strands of her hair. Would Monica think her rude if she left? She didn't really care. She looked for her jacket among the coats on the bed. What a waste buying the new black chiffon dress she was wearing.

She found her jacket, went downstairs, and slipped out quietly. She would call Monica tomorrow and explain that she had a headache and had thought it better not to bother with good-byes. Monica would probably be insulted, not invite her again, but so what? It was much more fun staying at home with the children.

Back at home she undressed slowly, wondering why on earth three hours previously she had painstakingly applied such a careful makeup and looked forward so excitedly to Monica's dreary gathering. What had she expected? Prince Charming, not a boring doctor with bad breath.

She felt depressed. Girls like Susan set the pace now with their lithe bodies. Face up to it, Linda, she thought, you've had your best years. You gave them to David. You've got two children. You're divorced. You have to settle for second best now.

She was lonely at night. Once, briefly, it had crossed her mind to phone Paul, but common sense had prevailed. Maybe she had made a mistake divorcing David. Maybe she *should* have given him another chance. But no, she was right, this was better than living a lie with David.

She fell into a troubled sleep.

An hour later the phone woke her.

'Hello.' Her voice was sleepy.

'Are you trying to avoid me?'

'What?' Her mind was still sleep-filled.

'I leave messages for you, you don't return my calls. You ignore me tonight and then just run off. I want dinner with you tomorrow night, no excuses.'

'Yes, Jay.' Her voice was weak.

'I'll pick you up at eight, and no calls to say you can't make it. I've phoned you three times.'

She didn't know what to say.

'All right, tomorrow at eight,' he said after a short pause. 'And wear that black dress you had on tonight, it looks great.'

Suddenly everything seemed bright again. Jay Grossman was certainly not second best.

* * *

Eventually Conrad returned. He had been gone an hour and a half, and Claudia, bored with the magazines and being kept waiting, was a little testy. She covered her irritation with a smile.

He was drunk. He grabbed hold of her, his fleshy hands feeling her body through her thin dress.

She wriggled away. This wasn't the way she had it planned.

'Aren't we going upstairs?' she asked.

His breath, a mixture of strong garlic and Scotch, enveloped her as he replied, 'Sure – sure. Just want a little preliminary.' He forced his hand inside the neckline of her dress, grabbing her breasts with rough fingers.

'You're hurting me,' she complained, and then, 'Hey – you're tearing my dress.' She pulled away from him again, furious at the torn dress, but still smiling provocatively. 'Let' s go upstairs, lover,' she cooed. 'Let's have a great scene upstairs.'

'Take your clothes off first – I want to take a look at the goods I'm getting,' he said urgently.

It was obviously no use arguing with him. She'd fix him when she got him in the sack.

Slowly she peeled off sensuous folds of white jersey. Underneath she had on only a wisp of a garter belt and pale sheer stockings, her long legs emphasized by the exceptionally high heels she was wearing.

He lunged at her, falling to his knees and grabbing her around the waist. He sank his teeth into her stomach and bit hard.

She screamed with pain and kicked him away. 'You son of a bitch!'

He laughed, hollow loud rumbles.

She rubbed her stomach, her eyes glinting dangerously, her mouth a tight smile. So he wanted to play games, huh? Well, she knew a few of her own.

'Come on.' He lumbered to the door. She followed him. He pushed her up the stairs ahead of him, stroking her legs, trying to feel between them.

They reached the bedroom. It was very dark; she could hardly see a thing.

'Get on the bed,' he commanded.

She climbed onto a large circular bed, grimly thinking things were going to be different in the morning when this big slob was sober.

He switched on the lights – bright glaring lights that hit the bed at a hard angle. She noticed a huge mirror above the bed.

He climbed on top of her, not even bothering to remove his clothes, just unfastening his trousers.

'Open up, baby,' he said. 'Let's have some action.'

He used her brutally – slamming and grinding into her, and afterwards wanting it different ways, making her do it to him at every conceivable angle.

She worked hard. This was something he had to remember. It was funny, really. When she became famous, everyone would say she was an overnight discovery. How right they would be!

At last he was finished. Her body ached from his pressures. She was bruised and worn. She lay spread-eagled on the bed, too limp to move.

He was surprisingly full of life. 'Got a little thrill for you,' he said. 'Just stay where you are.'

He got off the bed and pressed a switch by the door. The mirror above the bed parted and slid easily in two, leaving a gap in the ceiling. A ring of smiling faces peered down at her from the gaping aperture.

She sat up, horrified.

'Just a few of my friends,' Conrad said easily. 'These two-way mirrors are a great gimmick for making a party go with a bang!' He guffawed. 'Pick out who you'd like next.'

A woman's face, grotesquely made up and old, said, 'How about me, Conrad? Can I have a turn with her? She seems to know what it's all about.'

A man's voice said, 'No, me next. Let me give her a real fucking.'

'Oh, God!' Claudia jumped off the bed.

'What's the matter?' Conrad asked. 'Don't you want to be in my movie?'

She stared at him, every instinct warning her to get out.

But to leave now – what use was that? That wouldn't get her on the silver screen.

'All right,' she said at last. 'All right, I'll stay, but this time you'd better mean it.'

'I mean it,' he said blandly.

Chapter Sixteen

David managed to get through the early part of the next week without trouble. Miss Field was, as usual, the perfect, quiet, unobtrusive secretary. Neither of them made any reference to the previous Sunday. Indeed, it was as if it had never happened.

David felt that maybe it had all been a bad dream, but some grim sense of foreboding warned him that it was true. The sooner he was rid of Miss Field, the better. Meanwhile, their relationship was exactly the same as before.

He decided to wait a couple of weeks, then get her transferred to another department, maybe with a raise. She wouldn't object to that.

Mr. Taylor of the Fulla Beans account was in town. David didn't relish the thought, but as usual he was elected to entertain him. Did these poor out-of-towners *never* get tired of the inevitable clip-joint nightclubs and the pathetic, blowsy hostesses? It seemed not. Once more David had to fix him up, this time with a big redhead called Dora. Dora laughed a lot and suggested that it would be a lot of fun if Burt Taylor *and* David accompanied her back to her bed.

Neither of them liked the idea. Burt, because he didn't want to share. And David, because he didn't want to know.

She was very insistent, and when Burt Taylor, eyes bulging at the thought of the show she was offering, started to think it wasn't such a bad idea after all, David became really fed up.

He managed to finally persuade them to go off on their own. How he hated this sort of entertaining. These nightclub scrubbers weren't for him. He returned to his hotel room and went to bed.

The week dragged. Wednesday afternoon he phoned to speak to his children. They had just got home from school and were having tea. Ana told him Mrs. Cooper was out.

He was sure Linda wouldn't mind if he dropped by to see them. Maybe she would let him stay for dinner. It was all a question of time with Linda. Eventually she would realize the only sensible thing was to take him back.

He told Ana he would be right over. She mumbled something in Spanish. He could hear the children's excited squeaks in the background.

He left the office in high humour, went to Hamley's store, and filled his arms with toys. He stopped at Swiss Cottage and bought flowers. By the time he arrived at the house, it was two hours later.

Linda answered the door tight-lipped and furious. She stood in the doorway. 'The children are being bathed,' she said coldly.

'All right, I can wait.' He offered her the flowers.

She ignored them. 'David, we have an agreement that you only visit the children at the weekend.'

'What difference does it make when I come? Are you going to penalize me because I want to see my kids?'

She stood back wearily. She didn't want to be unfair as far as the children were concerned – after

173

all, he *was* their father. 'Come in, but please don't do this again.'

'What do you mean? Don't visit my own children again?'

'No, David, I mean please keep to the agreed times.'

'You surprise me.' He shook his head. 'I never thought you would use Janey and Stephen as a weapon against me.'

Her eyes filled with tears at the injustice of what he was saying. 'But I'm not. I'm just trying to do what's best.'

He looked at her coldly. 'And you think it's best that two innocent young children should not be allowed to see their father.'

'You're twisting what I'm saying.'

'I'm not twisting anything. I'm just repeating you.' He thrust the flowers at her. 'Take these – or perhaps you would prefer to throw them out like you would me.'

She accepted the flowers. 'I'll see if bathtime is finished.'

'Can I have permission to go upstairs and see them in the bath?' His voice was acid.

'Of course.'

Stephen stood at the top of the stairs, scrubbed and clean in striped pyjamas. 'Daddy!' he yelled.

Linda heard the cry of joy downstairs. She glanced at her watch. It was six o'clock. Maybe she should call Jay and tell him she couldn't keep their date. She felt so confused. David's attitude toward her was so unfair. He acted as if the whole thing was her fault.

He came downstairs, Janey cuddled in his arms, Stephen clinging to his hand. He fetched the packages from the car, and the children yelled with excitement.

Linda shut the door of the living room and left them all together. She went upstairs and lay down on the bed. She had thought the most painful part of divorce was over, but when you have children, it's never over. There's always a small questioning voice – 'Why doesn't Daddy live here anymore? When can Daddy come back? Do you love Daddy?'

She tried to contact Jay. He was out.

After an hour she went downstairs. With a forced smile she said, 'Come along – time for bed. School tomorrow.'

Stephen glared at her. 'Oh, Mummy!'

Janey started to cry.

David said, 'How about ten more minutes?'

'Please, Mummy,' Janey begged.

'Oh, OK – but no longer.' She glanced again at her watch. It was past seven, and Jay was due at eight. She didn't want him and David to meet. She wished she could find Jay and put him off. Not that she wanted to, but she really didn't feel like going out now.

After another twenty minutes the children were at last safely in bed with David reading them stories. By the time he came downstairs it was a quarter to eight. His mood was cordial. 'I could do with a drink.'

She was nervous. She had a perfect right to go out on a date, but she instinctively knew David wouldn't like it.

He poured himself a Scotch. 'You know, Stephen's a very bright lad. We must have a serious talk about his future.'

She pulled herself together. 'Yes, we must, but not now. I have to get changed.' Her voice became defiant. 'I'm going out.'

'That's nice.' There was a silence, then he added, 'Pretty cushy life you've got.'

Her voice was controlled. 'I beg your pardon?'

'Well, you know, no worries, nice house. I foot all the bills, and you can just run around doing what you like.'

'I don't run around and you know it.'

'Come off it. You're an attractive woman, a divorcee. Any man knows he's on to a good thing – a free lay is always popular. You must have dozens of offers. Why I bet—'

Her cheeks blazed. 'Get out! Get out of here!'

He put his drink down calmly. 'What's the matter? Don't try to tell me you're not getting it.'

'Please go, David. Right now.'

He sauntered to the door. 'All right, all right, don't get excited. I won't hang around to mess up your date. I'll get back to my hotel room – don't worry about me, just have a good time.'

When he reached the front door, she slammed it in his face.

He climbed into his car angrily. Thoughtless bitch! She was as bad as Claudia. They were all the same, all bitches trying to grab you by the balls and squeeze everything out of you.

He drove around the block and then came back and parked a few houses away. May as well wait and see who she was going out with.

* * *

Jay was a few minutes late, but hardly enough for Linda to recover. He found her in tears.

'I can't go out,' she sobbed.

He put his arm around her. She leaned her head against his chest and told him a jumbled account of what had happened.

He was sympathetic. 'You must talk to your lawyer first thing tomorrow. You can get a court order to stop him bothering you – he has set times to see the kids, and he'll have to stick to them.'

'I just thought it would be so mean of me not to let him see the children.'

'That's how he *wants* you to feel. He's probably had enough screwing around and decided to come back. His only way of getting at you is through the kids.'

'Do you think so?'

'Sure, listen, Linda – I'm experienced in these things. He blew a beautiful setup with you. You're not some little ding-a-ling – you're a lovely woman, and I bet he wants you back.' He paused and then asked casually, 'How do you feel about him?'

She was thoughtful. 'I don't know. I don't love him or anything like that. It's just that in spite of his insults, I do feel sorry for him. After all, I have the house and the children, and what does he have?'

'Hey, whoa, baby, you're starting to think like he *wants* you to think. He chose, didn't he?'

She nodded. 'You're right.'

'Good. At least you're starting to realize I'm always right!' He laughed. 'Now, go upstairs, powder your nose, put on your black dress, and let's go.'

She smiled. 'Yes, Jay.'

He took her to Annabel's. They dined elegantly. Jay entranced her with amusing stories about the film and the location in Israel. He told her about his children – there were three of them, one by his first wife and two by his second.

'Beautiful blond Californians,' he said wryly. 'I don't get to see them too much. Lori hated children.'

'How old are they?'

'Caroline's the eldest, she's fifteen – a real cuckoo kid. Lives in San Francisco with Jenny, my first wife. Then there's Lee, he's ten, and Lance, who's nine. They've got a great stepfather now, and I see them whenever I'm in LA.'

'I've never been to America. Is it as glossy as it all looks on the screen?'

He laughed. 'I guess you could say Hollywood is pretty glossy – personally, the only thing I really like there is the weather.'

After dinner they were joined by friends of Jay's, also in the movie business.

It was a lovely evening. Jay took Linda home in his chauffeured studio car and kissed her on the cheek.

'How about Saturday?' he asked.

'Yes,' she replied quietly.

'I'll call tomorrow. And don't forget, get on to your lawyer first thing.'

'I will.'

They smiled at each other. She let herself into the house and watched him through the window as he climbed back into the car. She liked him a lot.

* * *

Claudia buried herself in bed at her apartment. She huddled beneath the covers, bruised, used, and frightened to face anyone.

The day after the debacle with Conrad she called her agent and told him everything was fixed, and that he would be hearing from the studio. Then she took a variety of pills and slept, or tried to.

Claudia was not naive. There had been many men, many different scenes, the blue movies. But never anything so degrading as the evening at Conrad's house. When she closed her eyes, visions of evil, smiling faces swept before her. All the things they had made her do raced through her thoughts. She could still feel their hands. Her body screamed from the aches of sexual misuse.

She stayed beneath the covers, not eating, ignoring the telephone, inert and numb for several days.

Nobody cared, nobody came. If she died it would probably be months before they discovered her. Where were all her so-called friends?

At last she forced herself to get up. She was thin and white. She dressed and went out. The people in the street disgusted her. She went to see Giles. He was away in Majorca. She returned home and hacked off all her tawny glorious hair with her nail scissors. Then she slipped back into bed and, this time, slept.

When she woke the next day she felt much better. She opened some cans and ate. She was horrified to see what she had done to her hair. It stuck out at all angles and looked a mess. She read the papers and magazines that had piled up by the front door and called her agent.

No, he hadn't heard yet. Had she read that Conrad was getting married?

She grabbed the papers again. There it was – Conrad Lee, sixty-two years old, famous producer, to marry twenty-year-old model and ex-debutante Shirley Sheldon.

Shirley Sheldon! Claudia gasped in amazement. Shirley Sheldon! Ex-fiancée of the Honourable Jeremy Francis, ex-stripper. It couldn't possibly be true. Shirley was a phony debutante only interested in getting on in life. She had only hooked up with Jeremy because he had a title.

Claudia supposed she was going for Conrad's money and fame. But what on earth could *he* see in *her?* She wasn't *that* pretty, she had a lousy figure, and she was a dreary bore. The old schmuck must reckon she really was a debutante. What a laugh! Why, she had introduced them. She remembered Shirley coming to her party and having that great suntan. She must have got it in Israel. What a cow! Where had she been the other night? Didn't he involve his fiancée in his orgies? And if not, why not?

She read the article again. The wedding was set for that same day. She just couldn't believe it. Thin Shirley Sheldon, certainly not an ex-debutante, certainly not twenty.

'Ha!' she snorted. It was all too much.

On sudden impulse she raced to the phone book and looked up the Honourable Jeremy. She found his number and dialled quickly.

He was home, stammering and unsure as ever. 'I s-s-say, Claudia, how nice,' he said, after she announced herself.

'Are you going to Shirley's wedding?' she asked bluntly.

'I should jolly well s-s-say so, wouldn't want to miss that – w-w-hat?' He chortled happily.

'I thought we might go together,' she said casually. 'It's about time we saw each other again.'

'I say, what a good idea. S-s-shall I fetch you?'

She smiled. It was too easy. 'Terrific – what time?'

'If the reception s-s-starts at s-s-six, I think I should come for you at five-thirty.'

'Marvellous, Jeremy.' She gave him her address and hung up. What an idiot he was.

She spent the afternoon at the hairdresser and emerged with a whole new look. Her hair, short like a boy's, sleek, with long sideburns. Fortunately it was the look of the moment. Anyway, all the top models were wearing it. It went well with the ultrashort, skimpy gold shift she chose to wear.

Jeremy was impressed. 'I s-s-say, old girl, you look absolutely super!' he said, when he called for her.

She fixed him a strong martini and noticed his bad complexion was still the same. She resisted a strong temptation to ask him if he ever got laid.

'So good old Shirley's finally making the wedding-bells scene,' she said, sipping her martini and exhibiting a great deal of leg as she sat in the big armchair opposite him.

His eyes bulged. 'Yes. I'll s-s-say.'

'Whatever happened with you two?'

'Well' – he waved his long skinny arms about – 'she's a s-s-s-super girl, great fun and all that, but she s-s-said she needed someone more mature.' He took a few gulps of his drink, his Adam's apple bobbing rhythmically. 'We're s-s-still great pals,' he added lamely.

'Just as well,' Claudia said briskly. 'After all, she's so much older than you.'

'She is?' Jeremy looked surprised.

'I don't want to give away any secrets. I mean she looks after herself so well – but after all, how long can she go on fooling everybody?' Claudia shook her head wisely, and Jeremy stared at her, his mouth hanging open inanely. 'Shall we go?' she asked brightly, jumping up and smoothing her dress down.

'Er – yes.' Jeremy got up too.

He was very tall and ungainly – a real chinless wonder, Claudia thought. It was no surprise Shirley had ditched him for Conrad. At least Conrad had a certain grotesque style.

Jeremy drove a shiny red MG. It was very uncomfortable, he had to cram himself behind the wheel.

'Why don't you get a bigger car?' she asked. After all, his parents were supposed to be loaded.

'Oh, this little bus really gets me around,' he said proudly. 'Wouldn't s-s-swap this one in.'

He drove badly, jerking the clutch, cutting up other drivers without even noticing, and racing cars at the traffic lights.

Claudia felt sick by the time they arrived. She needed a fast drink. What a joy it would be to see Shirley's and Conrad's faces when they saw her. *Quelle surprise!*

* * *

David sat in his car smoking a cigarette. He didn't have to wait long before a sleek black chauffeur-

driven limousine glided to a halt in front of his house –
well, Linda's house. A man emerged. David was too
far away to recognize him. He swore under his breath
and edged his car a little nearer, but it was too late,
the man had already gone inside.

Well, Linda was certainly doing all right for
herself. The man, whoever he was, obviously had
money. Women were such schemers. They couldn't
wait – here they were divorced only a few weeks, and
there was Linda going out and living it up. She
probably had this sucker all lined up! Bitch! She was
no better than Claudia.

He waited impatiently for them to come out. They
were certainly taking their time, probably having a
quick one in the living room. He contemplated going
in and punching the man – whoever he was – on the
nose. But she probably wouldn't let him in anyway.

She would pay for this when he took her back. At
the rate she was going, maybe he wouldn't even want
her back.

He sat, immersed in his thoughts, until they finally
came out. The man, the bastard, had his arm around
her. The chauffeur jumped out and opened the door
for them. They climbed in, the chauffeur got back in
the car, and they slid off.

David set off in pursuit, keeping a discreet
distance between the cars. It was unfortunate for him
that at Swiss Cottage the chauffeur decided to skip
through a yellow light, and David, following him on
red, was stopped by a policeman on a motorcycle. He
had to produce his licence and insurance, and the
policeman gave him a lecture on dangerous driving.
Of course, by the time he was free to go, their car had
long vanished into the night. Pangs of hunger didn't

help his mood. He hated eating on his own, but at this hour there seemed no alternative. He decided to go somewhere cheerful, and he headed for Carlo's.

It was packed, as usual. Lots of bright-looking females in their most startling outfits, and the actors, photographers, and men about town who were their escorts for the night.

The headwaiter told him, with a phony sad shake of his head, that it would be at least two hours before he could squeeze a table for one in. David slipped him money, and the waiter became a little brighter about his prospects. He asked David to wait at the bar, and he would see what he could manage.

David ordered a Scotch on the rocks and surveyed the scene. He couldn't help thinking about the last time he had been here with Claudia. He wondered what she was doing now, but found he didn't really care. If it wasn't for her, he would be at home with his wife now.

A woman was staring at him. He stared back. She had mounds of silver-blond hair piled on top of her head, and she wore a white mink coat. Her face looked familiar. She was with two men who were in deep conversation – loud old Americans – one was wearing cowboy boots.

She sat very still. Cool, beautiful, and remote from her companions.

Suddenly David remembered her. It was Lori Grossman. He put his drink down and went over to her table. 'Hello, Lori,' he said, and then by way of jogging her memory, 'David Cooper. Remember me?'

Her smile was small, sensuous, as she extended an elongated whiter-than-white hand. 'David. How nice.'

The two men stopped talking. She introduced the elder one – he must have been all of seventy – as Marvin Rufus, her husband.

David looked surprised. Whatever happened to Jay?

'Sit down – have a drink,' Marvin said and immediately resumed his conversation with the other man.

Lori slipped off her white mink coat, revealing black lace, cut to a low V. She had small but perfect breasts. She was wearing no bra.

'I ditched Jay,' she said in answer to his unspoken question. 'He was a real cheap bastard.' She adjusted a fabulous diamond bracelet clamped around her thin wrist. 'Marvin knows how to treat a woman…' She trailed off, her pale, frosty, aquamarine eyes staring hungrily into his.

This one was ready! David congratulated himself on being so attractive to women. She was eating him up with her eyes! 'Linda and I are divorced,' he said. 'It just didn't work out.'

'Yeah, I know,' she drawled.

'You know?' he said, surprised.

She smiled. 'A little birdie told me. And I suppose *you* know that my darling peachy ex is dating your ex. Isn't that cosy?'

'Jay is taking out Linda?' He couldn't believe it.

'That's right, honey.' She moved closer to him, and he felt a sudden pressure from her leg under the table. His hand touched a silky thigh. She couldn't wait!

Marvin and the other man talked on, something about market prices in London, and would the pound be devalued.

'How long are you here for?' he asked.

'Just a couple of days,' she drawled.

That would be long enough. If Jay was knocking off Linda, he might as well grab a piece of Lori. She was obviously ready, willing, and able.

Under the table his hand crept further up her leg, reaching smooth skin above the stocking top.

'Are you meeting someone?' she asked.

He shook his head.

'You must join us then. Marve won't mind. He'll be talking business for hours.'

In a few minutes their table was ready. True to what Lori had said, her husband continued his marathon conversation with the other man, barely pausing to eat.

Lori ate like a sparrow, nibbling small pieces of steak, picking at a salad. Then the music started, and David asked her to dance. She was very tall, her bird's nest of hair making her even more so.

'Well?' he said when they were on the dance floor. The prospect of messing up this spectacular piece of aloofness was exciting him.

She felt his excitement and pressed closer.

'Marve will want to go gambling when we leave here. I'll say I'm too tired, and you'll offer to take me to the hotel. We have separate suites. He won't disturb us.'

He gripped her to him hard. He could feel her bones as she ground her body to the sound of the music.

'What if it doesn't work?' he asked.

'It will work.' She gave a low laugh. 'It always has before.'

Jay called Linda on Thursday and Friday as he had promised. Hearing from him each day gave her a feeling of well-being. He made her feel alive and attractive again.

She rushed around the shops searching for a suitable dress to beguile him with on Saturday night. Everything seemed to have been made for flat-chested seventeen-year-olds. She finally settled for a very simple white crepe shift, much too expensive, but beautifully cut. She spent the day absorbed in her children, taking them for a long walk on the heath and letting them ride on the donkeys. She loved the kids, and with Jay in her life she seemed to love them even more.

She took her time getting ready for him – long, hot scented bath, white crepe dress, a few pieces of good jewellery. She couldn't stop herself from thinking about him making love to her. Did he want to? He obviously liked her a lot. Would he make a pass at her tonight?

Make a pass – what a juvenile thought. She was a divorced woman with two children, not a teenager on a second date.

Would he want to sleep with her tonight? That was more like it. She wanted him, she needed him. It had been a long time. Finally she was ready, and he was, as usual, on time.

'You look lovely,' he said. 'You don't mind if we stop at a party for a few minutes? Business.'

The party was in Belgravia, an elegant pre-Victorian house complete with butler and maid at the door.

Linda was immediately intimidated. She glanced around the luxurious living room and recognized several well-known faces. The place seemed to be filled with stars and beautiful young girls. Jay knew everyone. He moved around, greeting people, while she trailed miserably behind him, feeling out of place and suddenly plain.

To top it all, a gorgeous blond whom she recognized as Susan Standish put her arm around him intimately and whispered loud enough for her to hear, 'You bastard! How dare you leave before I woke up this morning!'

Jay pushed the girl away, laughing easily.

Linda turned and walked across the room. Nobody seemed interested in talking to her. It was one of those parties where everyone was a 'somebody' in the film industry, and unless you were a 'somebody' or a beautiful young starlet, nobody wanted to know.

She found a chair and sat down. What a fool she had been. Jay wasn't interested in her, he was probably just sorry for her. She sat brooding. After all, he was a big director, he had the pick of all the girls in London. What could she offer him that he couldn't get more brightly packaged elsewhere?

He was heading in her direction. She turned on a bright smile, mustn't let him see she was upset – embarrass him, what for? There was nothing between them.

'Why did you rush off?' he asked, his eyes faintly amused. 'You left me in the clutches of a female would-be star – always in hot pursuit of us poor old directors. Why didn't you stay and protect me?'

She felt like saying, 'You slept with her last night, what do you expect?' Instead she just smiled and said, 'I don't know. I thought I'd sit down for a while.'

'We can go in a minute. I had to put in an appearance, otherwise Jan would never let me forget it.' He pointed to a striking woman in her forties, their hostess.

They left soon after and dined at a small French restaurant in Chelsea. Before they were halfway through their meal he asked her what was wrong.

Linda was bad at concealing her feelings, and her manner with Jay had become almost stilted. 'Nothing.' Inexplicably she found her eyes filling with tears.

He changed the subject. 'Let's take the kids out tomorrow. I'm looking forward to meeting them.'

She couldn't think of an excuse. 'All right.' She nodded numbly. 'Would you mind if I went home now? I've got a headache.'

He looked surprised but didn't question her. He paid the check and they left.

Conversation was sparse travelling back to Finchley. Linda found the presence of the chauffeur sitting faceless in the front a deterrent.

At the door she offered Jay her hand and he shook it gravely. 'I'll see you and the kids about twelve tomorrow. We'll take them to lunch,' he said.

She nodded listlessly. In the morning she would phone and cancel.

* * *

The wedding reception was crowded.

'Steer me to the bar. I need a drink!' Claudia said at once.

'I s-s-say, shouldn't we try to find them first?' Jeremy stuttered, looking vacantly around.

'No, let's get a drink.'

They headed for the bar. Claudia had a fast glass of champagne and felt better. She surveyed the crowd, a lot of Shirley's pseudo society friends and a group of American film people.

'Dreary-looking bunch,' she commented sharply.

Jeremy looked at her vaguely.

A waiter passed with a tray of canapés, and she grabbed a few. 'Ugh – lousy food!' she exclaimed. 'A bit of dried-up old sausage meat, sort of like the bridegroom!' She giggled and gulped down some more champagne.

Two tall, thin, slightly less acned replicas of Jeremy approached them. 'J. Francis, old chap,' one of them announced loudly, clamping his hand firmly on Jeremy's shoulder and surveying Claudia. 'How are we, then?'

'Oh, h-h-hello, Robin.'

Robin released his grip on Jeremy. 'Who's your lovely lady?'

Jeremy waved his arms about. 'Er, Claudia P-P-Parker – this is Robin Humphries.'

'Lord Humphries, old boy. Let the girl know who she's talking to.' He smiled at Claudia, revealing a line of crooked nicotine-stained teeth.

She smiled back. She was sipping her fourth glass of champagne.

The other young man pressed anxiously forward. 'I'm Peter Fore-Fitz Gibbons.' he said.

'I say, C-C-Claudia,' – Jeremy edged between her and Robin and Peter – 'we really should go and look for S-S-Shirley and her h-h-husband.'

'Whatever you say, lover.' She winked at the two young men. 'See you later. Keep it up.'

They exchanged puzzled looks.

'Funny girl, eh?' Robin said.

'Must be funny to be out with old Jeremy,' Peter agreed.

They watched her as she swayed across the room.

'Wouldn't mind a slice,' Robin said.

'Yes,' agreed Peter.

Claudia spotted Shirley. She made her way over fast. 'Shirley! You dark horse!' She stood firmly in front of her, one hand balancing a glass of champagne, the other holding onto Jeremy.

Shirley didn't bat an eyelid. She smiled politely. 'Claudia, darling, such a surprise! So glad you could make it, and Jeremy, poppet.' She stood on tiptoe while he placed a sloppy kiss on her cheek. 'Divine to see you both.'

'Where's the bridegroom?' Claudia asked, her words slurring slightly.

'He's around somewhere,' Shirley said brightly. 'Love your hair style, darling. Wish I could get away with such a harsh cut.'

Claudia smiled. 'I'm sure you could.'

Jeremy stammered, 'Jolly good show, this whole thing.'

Both girls ignored him.

'Conrad was telling me about the fun you had the other night,' Shirley said, her voice sugary.

Claudia gave her a sharp look. 'Yes, I thought *you* would be there.'

Shirley giggled softly. 'Why be there, when I can see the film?'

'What film?' Claudia's voice became harsh.

'Oh, Conrad always takes a film of those evenings.' Shirley smiled triumphantly. 'Didn't you know, it's his hobby, actually. You must come over one night, and we'll show it to you.'

Claudia stared at her, a horrible sinking feeling in her stomach. She knew Shirley wasn't lying.

'Well, darling,' Shirley continued, 'you did say you wanted to be in his movie.' With a tinkling laugh she turned away to greet another guest.

Claudia stood there, furious and burning. That son of a bitch!

Jeremy said, 'I say, old girl, everything s-s-super?'

She snatched her arm away. 'Shut up, asshole.'

'What,' he spluttered, looking hurt.

'Nothing.' She finished the last of her drink and handed him the empty glass. 'Get me some more, will you?'

She had seen Conrad. He was joking and laughing with an elderly couple.

She swayed over. 'Hey, man,' she said in a loud voice. '*Congratulations.*'

His piercing eyes swept over her with disinterest. Shirley walked over and attached herself protectively to his arm.

Claudia smiled at Shirley. 'He's a lousy lay – but then, I hear you are too, so that makes it cosy.'

The elderly couple exchanged glances and edged away. Jeremy appeared at that moment with a fresh glass of champagne.

Claudia took it and held it up to them. 'Here's to a couple of beat-up old fucks!'

People nearby were turning to stare.

Conrad said in a low, controlled voice, 'Get the hell out of here, cunt.'

Claudia smiled. 'My pleasure, cocksucker.' She took hold of a startled Jeremy's arm. 'Come on – let's split from this wake.'

A scarlet Jeremy exited with her.

Outside she started to laugh. 'Wasn't that funny? Wasn't that too much?!'

Jeremy stood there, his face a bright embarrassed red. 'I s-s-say, Claudia, how could you—'

'How could I what, man? It was only a giggle.' She suddenly flung her arms around him and kissed him, forcing his stiff lips open with her tongue.

'Come on, let's go back to my place and have some fun.'

Jeremy was reluctant to go, secretly wanting to return to the wedding reception and apologize. But Claudia insisted. 'I'll show you what it's all about, baby,' she whispered. 'I'll give you a trip you'll *never*forget.'

Back at her apartment, she fixed strong drinks and turned on the record player full blast.

Jeremy sat rigid and unsure of himself, while she danced around the room undulating her body and peeling off her dress.

She didn't take much notice of him as she got carried away with the music. She danced and caressed her own breasts, then, suddenly ready for him, she came over to where he sat and began to pull his clothes off.

He started to object.

'What are you – a faggot?' she screamed.

He got up and bolted for the door, running down the stairs like a startled rabbit.

Claudia followed him, yelling insults, but he didn't come back. In her drunken haze she was amazed. It was the first time a man – well, whatever he was – had turned her down. He had to be gay; those chinless-wonder types usually were.

She went back into the apartment and swigged from the Scotch bottle. Lousy faggot! How dare he refuse her. Probably couldn't do it. She giggled, and then her eyes inexplicably filled with tears. What was her life all about? Where was she getting? It didn't seem to be very far. All she wanted was to be a star. Was that asking so very much?

Tears rolled down her cheeks. She turned the music even louder, then lay on the floor by the speakers. The volume of the music excited her. She started to manipulate her own body – if that crazy skinny fag couldn't satisfy her, then she would just have to do it herself.

Before she could complete the job she fell into a deep drunken sleep, her snores mingling with the sound of John Lennon singing 'I'm a Loser'.

* * *

True to what Lori had said, after dinner Marvin immediately announced he wanted to gamble. The four of them stood in a huddle on the pavement in front of the restaurant.

'Wanna come and be my lucky charm?' Marvin asked Lori.

She wrapped her mink coat tightly around her and shook her head.

Cowboy Boots, anxious to be off, stamped around.

'Well, I guess I'll just play a little craps, then,' Marvin said.

'I'll see Lori back to the hotel if you like.' David quickly seized the opportunity.

'That's mighty nice of you,' Marvin boomed. He kissed Lori on the cheek. 'All winnings for you, sugar.' And with a brief handshake to David, he and Cowboy Boots were away in a cloud of cigar smoke and resonant Texan drawls. He was obviously a trusting husband. Either that or he couldn't care less.

Lori laughed. 'Didn't I tell you?'

They walked around the corner to his car, and Lori whispered to him, 'Are you big? I only like big men.'

In the car she acted like a bitch in heat, grabbing for him immediately. He was proud of what he had to offer. Quickly he drove to the hotel.

Lori swept through the lobby, haughty and imperial, her white mink drawing envious stares from women. She stopped and greeted an actor she knew. The man gave David an amused look.

Her suite was on the sixth floor, very luxurious, furnished in opulent blue and silver. She threw her mink casually over a chair. 'Make yourself a drink, honey,' she drawled. 'I'm just going to put on something more comfortable.' Her dialogue was straight out of a Hollywood movie! He opened a bottle of champagne conveniently on ice and poured two glasses. This was the life! A beautiful woman in beautiful surroundings, champagne, what more could a man ask?

She came back soon – wearing a sheer black negligee, her hair still piled high. He handed her a glass of champagne and she took a small sip, then lay down on the sofa, the negligee falling back slightly, revealing milky-white thighs.

He didn't feel quite ready. She held out her arms to him. 'Come to baby, honey,' she drawled.

He put his drink down and went to her.

'There's a silk robe in the bathroom,' she purred. 'Why don't you get out of your clothes and be comfortable like me.'

He did feel a bit restricted, and the setting seemed too perfect to start struggling out of his clothes all over the floor.

He kissed her on the mouth, tasting her lipstick, and then went to the bathroom and put on the robe she had suggested. It was paisley silk, probably her husband's. He admired his masculine figure in the mirror, not bad for forty!

She was waiting for him, draped across the sofa, looking like a *Vogue* advertisement. He took her in his arms.

She put her hands inside his robe, scratching his chest gently with talon-like fingernails.

He stroked her body. She was very thin, with small hard breasts and extended large nipples. An exciting body – not soft and warm like Linda, nor curvy and exciting like Claudia. But very sensuous, all the same. Like a smooth white snake.

He parted her negligee. Her legs were exceptionally long, crowned at the top by a small mound of silver-blond hair, matched perfectly to the hair on her head. She opened them slowly, her hands moving around his back, digging her nails into him, pulling him closer.

With surprise he realized he wasn't yet ready. To distract her from this fact he moved his head to her breasts and started to kiss them.

She moaned softly, digging her nails even harder into his back. After a few minutes she grew impatient, and her hands travelled down his body. Her eyes were closed, but they snapped open suddenly when she felt him.

'What's the matter, honey?' she purred, a slight edge to her voice. 'This is real Georgia pussy!'

Embarrassed, he said, 'It's nothing, just give me a moment.'

Annoyed, she closed her eyes again, this time her hands working on him, pulling, stroking, kneading.

'Come on, sugar,' she pleaded, 'this little snatch is waiting for you!'

His physical reaction was nil. This was a nightmare, something that had never happened to him before. He grew panicky, conjuring up every erotic picture he could think of.

Nothing, absolutely nothing.

He tried to remember the last time he had had sex. Mousy Miss Field, his horrifying secretary. Desperately he thought of the evening he had spent with her.

Suddenly it was all right. He felt himself swelling, growing big, bigger.

Lori sighed with pleasure. 'That's beautiful, honey.' She wrapped her long pale legs around him as he started to enter her, forcefully, powerfully. He would show her!

He drove into her. Strong, brutal thrusts.

She squealed with delight. 'Ooh – ooh – that's great, honey – that's wild – ooh – don't stop – don't stop.' Her voice changed. 'Why have you stopped?'

He didn't reply. He was too overcome with embarrassment. He had heard about this happening to other men, but not to him.

She was getting angry. Her sleek, sexy drawl turned shrill. 'What's the matter with you? Are we going to ball or not? If I want this sort of action, I can get it with my husband!'

He rolled off. 'I'm sorry.'

Furious, she sat up. '*You're* sorry.' She stood up too, her hard breasts and exotic nipples staring accusingly at him. 'Get the hell out of here. I've got to find myself a *real* man.'

Humiliated, he went to the bathroom and dressed.

When he came out she was on the phone purring, 'Sure, honey, in ten minutes' time will be fine.'

He let himself out feeling ashamed. What a terrible thing to happen, and why? He had fancied her strongly. It wasn't *her* fault. Although maybe it was. She made no secret of the fact that there were many men other than her husband.

He went to the bar and ordered a brandy. By the time he had finished it he had convinced himself it was *all* Lori's fault. Lousy bitch! She had castrated him with thoughts of all the other men. They were all the same, women. They all wanted to render you impotent in one way or the other.

On impulse he decided to give it another try that night. Not with Lori, of course. But what about Miss Field Mouse? She was quiet and inoffensive, and he was going to get rid of her anyway, so what harm one more bash?

He didn't even fancy her, so it would be real proof if he could make it with her.

He vaguely remembered where she lived. She was sure to be home, so he had another brandy and set off.

Hammering on her door, he found himself as hard as a rock.

She got out of bed to answer the door, clutching a woollen dressing gown around her. Lank brown hair, sallow pinched face. 'Mr. Cooper!' she exclaimed.

He pushed past her, taking his clothes off and dropping them on the floor. 'Get undressed,' he commanded.

Averting her eyes, she obeyed him.

He took her savagely, pinning her puny body to the floor.

There was nothing wrong with him!

Chapter Seventeen

Linda never did phone and cancel Jay the next morning. He arrived, took them out to lunch, and the children were captivated.

He told them stories, played with them, and then they all went to a movie.

In the evening he stayed at the house for a bacon-and-egg supper and Linda found herself unable to break off the relationship. She put Miss Susan Standish to the back of her mind and continued going out with Jay. She liked him, the children liked him, Janey especially. He was wonderful with them.

It became a routine to spend every Sunday together. Jay always thought of new things for them to do, and they looked forward to their day out eagerly. It was a good thing, because since David's last visit he had not been heard from. Linda was furious. It was a pleasure as far as she was concerned, but she thought it selfish and mean of David to completely ignore the children. They were constantly asking, 'When's Daddy coming?' 'Where is he?' If it hadn't been for Jay at weekends she was sure they would have been even more upset.

'Doesn't Daddy love us anymore?' Janey asked sadly one afternoon.

'Of course he does, darling,' Linda replied, hugging her little girl to her. 'He's just very busy.'

'I love Uncle Jay,' Janey said solemnly. *'He's* not too busy.'

So their relationship flourished, and at the end of a few weeks Linda found herself firmly in love with him. They went to the theatre, small intimate restaurants, large exciting parties, movies. In fact, they spent almost every night together and regularly every weekend. They went to the zoo, the park, museums and drives in the country.

He was amusing, attentive, interested in everything she did, but he never attempted more than a brief – almost brotherly – good-night kiss.

It started to drive her mad. Her body screamed out for some sort of attention. Whenever they danced, she would have to hold herself in tight check to prevent herself pushing her body intimately against him. When they kissed, she was in suspense waiting for him to go further. But he remained the perfect gentleman. Never touching her.

It reached a point where she decided she could go on no longer, and she resolved to bring it up at the next suitable moment.

The opportunity came sooner than expected. There was an end-of-film party at the studio. Linda was chatting to Jay and Bob Jeffries, the assistant director, when up marched Miss Standish. She was wearing the same white pants suit Linda had seen her in before. It suited her, complementing her glowing skin and tumbled blond hair.

'Jay, darling,' she murmured, 'can I have a little word with you?' She had sly eyes, a secret smile always present.

'What is it, Susan?' His tone was pleasant.

'Privately.'

Jay shrugged his shoulders at Linda and Bob and walked away with Susan.

Linda said, 'Is she in the film?'

Bob laughed. 'At the moment she is, but I've got a feeling she's going to land on the cutting-room floor.'

'Oh.' Linda quickly changed the subject. She didn't want Bob to think she was jealous.

Jay returned quite soon and didn't mention the incident, but Linda knew that as soon as they were alone she was going to bring it up.

After the party, joined by Bob Jeffries and his wife, they went to Annabel's. It was impossible to talk there, and on the drive home there was the ever-present chauffeur.

'You're very withdrawn tonight,' Jay said, his tone light.

She nodded.

'What's the matter?' He was concerned.

'I don't want to talk now,' she said, looking toward the chauffeur. 'Come in for coffee if you like.'

She had never invited him into her house when he took her home before; perhaps she should have.

She left him in the living room and went into the kitchen. Now that she had him there, what was there to say? It was all so difficult. There were no words that could really express the way she felt.

Absently she placed some chocolate biscuits on a plate and fixed coffee.

He was sitting reading the evening paper. She felt at a complete loss for words as she handed him his coffee.

He solved the problem for her by speaking first. 'I have to go back to Los Angeles in two weeks.'

'Oh.' She felt deflated.

He hesitated and then said, 'How about coming with me?'

'With you?' For a few pleasant seconds she considered the possibility, then reality hit her. 'That's impossible, Jay. I can't leave the children.'

'Bring the children. They'd love it.'

She shook her head. 'I can't take them out of school. Anyway—'

He cut her short. 'Linda, I'm not very good at this sort of thing. I've only ever said it to idiots before.' He got up nervously. 'Linda, I'm asking you to marry me.' He rushed on. 'I guess I love you. You're the most wonderful, warm, giving woman I've ever met. I know you've been burned once, and I know how you feel – but believe me, I'll try to make you happy. I'm not perfect. I've been involved with a lot of stupid broads – I've got a weakness for tall blondes I can't deny – but if you'll marry me, I think everything will work out, and I think we could make a wonderful life together.' He paused. 'Well?'

'Jay.' She whispered his name. 'Yes, Jay, yes, yes.'

He kissed her. 'Let's do it soon, like tomorrow. I can't wait for you much longer.'

She felt tears stinging her eyes. 'I love you.'

He stroked her hair, then let her go. 'Go to bed. I'll call you first thing. I'll arrange everything. The sooner the better, huh?'

She nodded. 'The sooner the better,' she murmured.

* * *

Claudia spent the days after Shirley and Conrad's wedding in a drunken stupor. She drank a full bottle of

Scotch a day, occasionally cramming her mouth with sleeping pills or tranquillizers until she reached a sort of happy oblivion. She didn't eat, wash, or dress, just wandered around the apartment in sordid naked splendour.

The phone rang but she never picked it up. One day the door buzzer rang so insistently that she was forced to answer it.

It was Giles. 'Christ!' He was aghast at her appearance. He bundled her into a dressing gown and made her drink black coffee until her eyes started to focus and she could talk.

'What kind of a trip have *you* been on?' he demanded.

She shook her head. 'I feel terrible.'

'You *look* terrible.'

'What day is it?'

'God, you've *really* been away. It's Monday.'

'Monday. I guess I went on a little bender.'

He surveyed the room, empty Scotch bottles, broken records, overturned furniture. 'I guess so. Who was the guy?'

She shrugged. 'No one. Just felt like getting stoned alone. What are you doing here anyway? Thought you were in Spain.'

'I've come bearing glad tidings. Your tits are world-famous.'

He produced a copy of Man at Play, one of the biggest-selling men's magazines in the States.

He opened it and showed her the centre fold-out. There she was in solid colour standing on her terrace with London silhouetted in the background, wearing the pink shirt which Giles had hosed with water, her perfect rounded breasts standing out firm and full, the nipples rigid and pointed.

He turned the page. There she was lying on her bed, black negligee, breasts escaping, mouth half-open, eyes half-closed.

The next page and the next page were all of her. The caption said *Beautiful London model and actress Claudia Parker shows us some of the better sights of Great Britain.*

'You're a big hit,' Giles said enthusiastically. 'They want us to do a whole new series of photos. They'll pay a bomb. Want us to fly to New York. Want you to meet Edgar J. Pool – owner of the magazine. This is your big chance, baby. *This* is successville.'

She studied the magazine. Why, oh why, had she cut her hair?

'When do we go?' she asked, her face lighting up.

'As soon as we get you into shape. You look scrawny as hell, and that hair – we'll have to get you a wig. Here, sign this.'

He thrust a paper at her which she signed without so much as a glance.

'I'm going to book you into a health farm for a week. You really need it. I reckon about ten days from now we can go. I'll let them know. They're really wild for you – want you to be Miss Playmonth of the Year. Baby, you and I are going to be rich!'

* * *

Was it the fifth or sixth night David had spent with Miss Field? He couldn't remember. He only knew it had become a habit to leave the office, eat dinner, have a few drinks, and then go hammering on her door.

She held a sort of morbid fascination for him. What was it that made sex with her so overpowering and exciting? It was certainly the most erotic experience he had ever had. She always crept to the door clutching her woollen dressing gown around her. He had to command her to undress. Then she took her clothes off reluctantly, revealing a thin, white, undernourished body. She was flat-chested, with flaccid nipples that didn't even harden to the touch. However, when he was in her, pounding away, she held him in a grip of steel, squeezing and pumping the life out of him. Giving him no rest, holding him in her like a vice.

He hated her, but he couldn't stop returning night after night.

During the day at the office neither of them mentioned it. She crept around quietly going about her business, mouselike as usual.

He wanted to break the habit.

A busty, provocative-looking girl called Ginny was doing an ad for his company. He manoeuvred an introduction, found her very attractive. She reminded him of a much sexier, more obvious version of Claudia.

He invited her out to dinner. She turned up in an almost topless, startling red dress. She had pink-and-white English skin and full pouty lips.

This was going to be all right, he decided.

During dinner she drank frozen daiquiris and giggled a lot. They danced, and her body was warm and bouncy. All the men in the restaurant were watching her, which made David feel good. At one point, during a vigorous dance, one full pink-and-white breast popped completely over the top of her dress, giving a delightful view of a pale brown nipple, pert and generous. She tucked herself back into her dress with an inane giggle.

David felt the time had come to take her back to his hotel. She put up little objection, and once there, it was an easy job to peel her out of the red dress.

She was wearing frilly pink panties, and her body was ripe. Her breasts were so big and bouncy and unbelievable that he had a sneaky suspicion that they weren't breasts at all, just a lot of silicone injections put together.

He couldn't do anything. There was no excitement.

Still giggling, she was given money for a taxi and sent home.

He went to bed, couldn't sleep, until at last he was forced to get up and visit Miss Field. By the time he got there his excitement was at such a peak that he hardly made it on top of her.

She had a strange power over him.

He tried with several other women, but each time the same result. His life began to revolve around Harriet Field.

He found out about her. She was thirty years old and had been with the firm for twelve years, working her way up from the typing pool to become his private secretary. There was no gossip about her. She kept herself to herself. She was the office nonentity.

When he went to her at night they never talked. He just told her what to do and she did it, whatever it was.

Sometimes, after sex, she asked him if he would care for coffee or tea. He would always say no, and as soon as he could summon the strength, get up and go.

He wondered what she thought about it all. Why did she never say anything? The whole thing was unnatural.

The next time, of course, was later that same evening. He arrived earlier than usual, and she was still up, clutching a skimpy cardigan around her nonexistent bosom. Automatically she started to undress.

It was the first time he had ever seen her get out of her clothes; usually it was just a nightgown and dressing gown.

There seemed to be layers of them. Skirt, cardigan, sweater, a vest (one of the most unattractive garments he had ever seen), salmon-pink bra, a slip, long woollen drawers, and thick stockings. Shivering slightly, she stood before him.

She was certainly a randy bitch, he thought, always prepared. Always creamed up and ready to go. Probably been frustrated for years.

Maybe he should make her wait for it tonight. She was already lying on the floor, opening pale, sluggish legs.

He couldn't make her wait. The burning desire he felt wouldn't let him. He ripped off his clothes hurriedly and crouched on top of her.

She heaved a big sigh and they were away.

Afterward she put on her dressing gown and started to tidy his clothes, piling them neatly together, ready for him to put on.

He lay watching her. She really was plain – it wasn't that she made the worst of herself, it was just that there was nothing one could do to improve her.

She noticed him looking and flushed. 'Tea or coffee, Mr. Cooper?'

'Both,' he said abruptly.

She turned to go into the kitchen, and he had a feeling she would bring him both if he didn't stop her.

'Sit down,' he said.

She sat hesitantly, crossing her feet at the ankles, clasping her hands on her lap in front of her.

'I want to talk to you,' he said.

They sat silently. After he had said he wanted to talk to her, he suddenly realized he didn't want to talk to her at all, he just wanted to go.

'It doesn't matter,' he said abruptly.

'Is something wrong, Mr. Cooper?'

'For God's sake, don't call me Mr. Cooper.'

She lowered her eyes. 'Yes, David dear.'

Christ, she acted like the vestal virgin. She became so coy and retiring.

He stood up, decisions filtering through his mind. He would fire her on Monday, and this was positively the last time.

Maybe he should hammer it into her once more since this was his last visit. 'Get across the table,' he said wearily.

* * *

Linda and Jay were married a week later at Hampstead register office. Quietly, with no fuss.

Linda's parents were present, surprised but happy. The children, dressed in their best clothes, were strangely subdued. A few friends of Jay's and a few of Linda's attended the ceremony.

209

Afterward they all went back to Jay's hotel suite and ate wedding cake and drank champagne. It was very small, very informal.

Soon Linda's parents said they should be starting the drive back to the country. They gathered together the children, who were going to stay with them, and said their good-byes.

Linda hugged Janey and Stephen to her. 'Mummy won't be away very long, and then we're all going to live together in a beautiful big house with a swimming pool in America.'

'Wow – a swimming pool!' Stephen said delightedly.

Janey was fighting back tears, her innocent chubby face concerned and worried. 'I hope the plane doesn't crash, Mummy.'

Linda laughed and hugged her. 'Don't be a silly baby.'

Jay picked up Janey and kissed her. 'You be a good little girl, and Mummy will be back before you know it.'

Janey looked at him with big brown eyes. 'Are you my new daddy?'

He nodded solemnly. Janey kissed him and scampered off to her grandparents. Soon the rest of the guests departed and they were alone.

Linda took off her hat and sighed. 'I hate leaving the children.'

Jay laughed. 'It's only for a couple of weeks. You don't mind if I have a little time alone with my wife?'

'No, I don't mind.' She smiled at him. 'I love you.'

There were several telegrams, one from Conrad and Shirley Lee, honeymooning in Mexico: *Congratulations. English wives are best.*

They don't want so much alimony. Love, regards, Conrad and Shirley.

A sarcastic one from Jay's fifteen-year-old daughter: *Best wishes, Daddy, on your fourth wife. Caroline.*

'She's a fresh kid,' he said grimly.

'Why do you say that?' Linda asked.

'I don't know.' He shrugged. 'I guess it's my fault, really. She's a tough little cookie – takes after her mother. I never spent any time with her, and Jenny didn't remarry so I suppose it's affected her, not having a father around.'

'I'd like to meet her,' Linda said quietly. 'Maybe when we're settled she could come and stay with us for a while.'

'Forget it.' He laughed brusquely. 'Her mother would never allow it. Anyway, she's not a child anymore. It's too late for me to start stepping into the picture.'

'She's only a teenager. I think we should try it.'

He kissed her. 'You're sweet.'

She smiled and changed the subject. 'I hope I've brought the right clothes for Jamaica. It's all been such a rush.'

'Are you sorry?'

'Sorry? What a ridiculous thing to say. Of course I'm not.'

'Let's have dinner up here. The car will be picking us up at six in the morning. We'd better get an early night.'

'That's a wonderful idea.' She yawned. 'I'm going to have a bath now.'

'Leave it to me. I'll order you something special.'

She went into the bathroom. Her two suitcases and makeup case were stacked neatly on luggage racks.

She hoped she wasn't going to be a big disappointment to Jay. He was used to such beautiful women. She remembered elegant, cool Lori.

Quickly she bathed, then unpacked a long blue silk nightdress and matching robe. It flattered her, plunging between her heavy breasts and swirling down to the floor clingingly. She brushed her thick auburn hair; it was growing, and reached to her shoulders. Her body and face were by no means perfect, but she was an attractive, sensuous-looking woman.

Jay had ordered more champagne, a delicious fish course, and thin slivers of perfect white chicken in a creamy mushroom sauce on a bed of rice. Then strawberries Romanoff and large goblets of Courvoisier brandy.

After dinner Linda felt gloriously happy. Jay made everything perfect. In the bedroom he undressed her slowly, and made love to her beautifully. Nothing frantic, nothing rushed. He caressed her body as though there was nothing more important in the world. He took her to the edge of ecstasy and back again, keeping her hovering, sure of every move he made.

She floated on a suspended plane, a complete captive to his hands and body.

He had amazing control, stopping at just the right moment. When it did happen it was only because he wanted it to, and they came in complete unison. She had never experienced *that* before, and she clung to him, words tumbling out of her mouth about how much she loved him.

Afterward they lay and talked.

'You're wonderful,' he said. 'You're a clever woman, making me wait until after we were married.'

'What?' She snuggled closer to him.

'I wanted you so much. But I knew if I made a wrong move I'd become just another guy on the make. I laid Lori the first time I saw her. She came for an interview, we locked the office door, and made it then and there. Can you imagine marrying a broad you screwed as soon as you met? That's what kind of schmuck I was until I met you, and realized what a real relationship could be.'

She kissed him. 'But weren't you worried if we'd – well – like each other in bed? I mean, why *didn't* you try before?'

'Because I wasn't about to take no for an answer.'

'But I might not have said no.'

He agreed. 'No, you might not have, but you're not the sort of woman to have an affair. You would have regretted it, and I would have become the bad one in your mind.'

'Oh.' She was amazed at how well he knew her. He was probably right. 'What about Susan Standish?' she asked accusingly.

'I'm a man, Linda,' he said simply. 'Don't expect me to make excuses. She was a nice girl, and I couldn't have you.'

Her eyes were closing. 'I love you, husband,' she murmured, and soon she was asleep.

* * *

The health farm wasn't too bad. It was a place to relax, to think and take stock. Claudia submitted her body to the care of experts, and within a few days her physical appearance was back to normal.

She spent her days between massage and therapy, sunning herself beside the luxurious swimming pool in the grounds. The early English sun was weak but restful. She daydreamed a lot of the time, imagining herself a star, a success. That was all she really wanted out of life.

Giles came to visit her. 'You look great!' he said enthusiastically. 'Just like the girl I used to know.'

He had correspondence from the magazine, eagerly awaiting her arrival.

'You've really made a big impression on *someone* there,' he said cheerfully. 'They can't wait. Planning promotions for you all over the place. They want to feature you big, kid.'

She was delighted. Maybe this was the opportunity she had been waiting for.

Soon she was ready to leave the health farm. Giles took her back to his studio flat in Chelsea. 'I've moved all your things out of the penthouse,' he told her. 'It's not a good scene for you. You'll stay with me until we go.'

She was pleased. Giles was taking her over, and she liked it.

They slept in a big sprawling bed like brother and sister, and during the day Giles took her shopping for new clothes. She bought a fabulous shiny ash-blond wig to cover her own cropped hair until it grew back.

He paid for everything. 'An investment,' he told her airily.

Eventually he decided they were ready to go, and he cabled the magazine.

He received a lengthy reply which stated that they had already sent the tickets. And *'Be Prepared. Big Welcome For Future Miss Playmonth. All Press Alerted. Party Planned for Tour Arrival.'*

Claudia was delighted. New York awaited her.

* * *

It was just no good. David could not break the habit of Harriet Field. He found it absolutely impossible to get an erection with any other woman.

He tried religiously, even going so far as to take a girl to a pornographic movie in the hope that that would excite him enough. The result was the girl got so worked up that when he couldn't satisfy her, she called him every filthy name she could think of.

He felt if he could only make it with someone other than Harriet Field, the spell would be broken. But it remained an impossible feat, and sex with Harriet got better and better.

He took to staying at her apartment all night, for now he found he had to have her in the morning too.

She became even more white and insipid-looking. Slowly she seemed to be draining the strength from him.

He would wake up in her cramped apartment, bad-tempered and uncomfortable. It was obvious that if he was going to continue this relationship he would have to make other arrangements about her living quarters. He didn't want to set her up in an apartment, but it seemed the only answer.

She never said anything to him when they weren't having sex, just kept well out of his way.

Usually he drove her to the office, dropping her a block away. She would huddle in her seat mouselike and silent.

He hated her, but he couldn't leave her. Was it never going to end, this mad animal desire he had for this wretched creature?

He hadn't seen his children for a long while. Too long. Somehow he felt ashamed to face them.

His life became one long round of work, into which he threw himself wholeheartedly. And sex with Harriet. He looked thin and haggard.

It's got to end soon, he reasoned. I'll just keep going until I've had so much of her it will be over.

He ignored everything else and concentrated on getting Harriet out of his system. This involved sleeping with her at every possible opportunity, and now, even at the office he would sometimes lock the door and take her quickly on the floor or across his desk. It didn't help. It just seemed to make her more exciting.

He plodded on, determined to finish the affair.

* * *

At London airport Claudia was besieged by photographers.

'Look this way.' 'Over here, Claudia.' 'Pull your skirt up, dear.' 'Let's see some leg.'

Claudia obliged. She was wearing a very short skirt with matching coat and clingy silk sweater.

Giles stood by watching. He knew he had made a smart move getting her to sign the personal management contract. Now he had fifty percent of her, and he had a hunch that fifty percent was going to mean an awful lot of money.

216

The Americans were about to discover a new sex symbol. She would bowl them over. In England she was just another little starlet. In America she had the potential to become a big star. Giles was sure of this. With the right exposure and the right publicity, she had it made.

Of course he would have to watch her closely, see she didn't drink too much, didn't get laid by the wrong people.

She smiled sexily at the photographers, head thrown back, lips parted, slanty green eyes shining. She blossomed even more in the limelight. Her bosom strained to escape the thin confines of her sweater, her legs were long and shapely.

'Come on, baby, we'll miss the plane,' Giles said at last.

She gave the photographers one last provocative pose, then took his hand, squeezing it firmly.

'This is a ball!' she exclaimed. 'I love it, baby. *Love* it!'

* * *

In another part of the airport Linda and Jay sat in a VIP lounge sipping coffee. Jay's was laced with a good stiff shot of whiskey. He hated flying and found the only way he could climb on a plane was to be mildly drunk.

Linda admired her wedding ring, a thin band of perfect diamonds. She could hardly believe how much she loved this man. After David, the thought of being able to pick up the pieces and start again had seemed impossible. Now, the ten years with David seemed almost nonexistent.

Jay took her hand. 'You look beautiful today.'

She smiled. 'Thank you.'

A stewardess arrived and told them it was time to board the plane. A lone photographer stopped them in the hall. 'Is it possible to have a picture, Mr. Grossman?'

'Sure.' Jay smiled amicably and put his arm around Linda.

She was surprised. 'Why do they want your picture?' she whispered.

'The studio usually arranges it. Another plug for the movie.'

'Oh.' She nodded wisely.

They sat in comfort on the plane, Jay taking furtive swigs out of a silver hip flask. Then the great engines began to roar, and the plane taxied gently off down the runway.

* * *

One morning David woke up in a particularly foul temper. His head ached, and the room smelled of stale sex – Harriet never seemed to open any windows. He reached for her at once, his physical feelings overcame anything else.

After satisfying himself, he felt even worse.

She made him coffee and gave him the morning paper. He smoked a cigarette and glanced at the paper. On the front page was Claudia. She faced the camera three-quarters on, bosom thrust out, hair long and wild, amused, knowing smile. She looked gorgeous, shapely legs disappearing into a short skirt.

Beautiful model and actress Claudia Parker (21) leaves for New York today. Miss Parker plans to discuss film offers. She is travelling with Giles

Taylor, well-known fashion and society photographer. Both deny a romance.

David felt anger that she should look so good and appear so happy. After he had left her he had imagined she would go to pieces, vanish from his life. But here she was on the front page, off to America, without, apparently, a care in the world.

Bitch! She had ruined his marriage.

He turned the page in a fury. Why couldn't she just have faded into oblivion?

There, on the next page, was a small picture of Linda with a man. She looked calm and smiling. The man held her arm protectively.

Mr. Jay Grossman, well-known Hollywood director, and the new Mrs. Grossman leave for a honeymoon in Jamaica. Mr. Grossman has just finished making *Besheba* here and on location in Israel.

Mrs. Jay Grossman – it was impossible. How dare she! He studied the picture intently, searching her face for signs of unhappiness, but there were none – she was serene and confident and very attractive.

How could she do it without telling him?

Then he remembered. Last week she had left three messages at the office for him to phone her, and he hadn't bothered to return her calls.

'Goddamn!' he swore angrily. He had always imagined that Linda would be available when he *did* decide to settle down. She would take him back. Harriet Field had delayed his thoughts about getting back with her. He had drifted into a sordid affair and everything else had been neglected. He hadn't even thought about seeing his children.

He felt trapped. What could he do? There was no Linda to save him now. The time had come to run.

Desperately he thought of the words of a children's song – *Run Rabbit – run rabbit – run run run* – and they repeated in his mind with an insistent monotony.

There were retching sounds coming from the bathroom. Soon Harriet came into the room. Unusual for her, she hadn't dressed yet, but was clutching her faded woollen robe around her.

She stood in front of him, white and wretched-looking. 'We are with child,' she stated blankly.

He stared at her in a panic. And slowly he realized it was too late to run – the trap had closed.

JACKIE COLLINS

There have been many imitators, but only Jackie Collins can tell you what really goes on in the fastest lane of all. From Beverly Hills bedrooms to a raunchy prowl along the streets of Hollywood; from glittering rock parties and concerts to stretch limos and the mansions of the power brokers – Jackie Collins chronicles the real truth from the inside looking out.

Jackie Collins has been called a "raunchy moralist" by the late director Louis Malle and "Hollywood's own Marcel Proust" by **Vanity Fair**magazine. With over 500 million copies of her books sold in more than 40 countries, and with some twenty-nine **New York Times** bestsellers to her credit, Jackie Collins is one of the world's top-selling novelists. She is known for giving her readers an unrivaled insider's knowledge of

Hollywood and the glamorous lives and loves of the rich, famous, and infamous! "I write about real people in disguise," she says. "If anything, my characters are toned down – the truth is much more bizarre."

Jackie Collins started writing as a teenager, making up steamy stories her schoolmates paid to devour. Her first book, **"The World is Full of Married Men,"** became a sensational bestseller because of its open sexuality and the way it dealt honestly with the double standard. After that came **"The Stud," "Sinners," "The Love Killers," "The World is Full of Divorced Women," "The Bitch," "Lovers And Gamblers," "Chances,"** and then the international sensation,**"Hollywood Wives"** – a #1 **New York Times** bestseller, which was made into one of ABC's highest-rated miniseries starring Anthony Hopkins and Candice Bergen.

"The Stud," "The World is Full of Married Men," and **"The Bitch"**were also filmed – this time for the big screen. And Jackie wrote an original movie, **Yesterday's Hero**, starring Ian McShane and Suzanne Somers.

Readers couldn't wait to race through **"Lucky,"** her next book – a sequel to **"Chances"** – and the story of Lucky Santangelo, an incredibly beautiful, strong woman, another **New York Times** number one. Oprah had one word for the book **"Lucky,"** and that was – **"Hot!"**

Next came the bad boys of Hollywood in the steamy **"Hollywood Husbands"** – a novel which kept everyone guessing the identities of the true-to-life Hollywood characters.

Jackie then wrote **"Rock Star"** – the story of three rock superstars and their rise to the top, followed by the long-awaited sequel to **"Chances"** and **"Lucky"** – **"Lady Boss"** – tracking the further adventures of the wild and powerful Lucky Santangelo as she takes control of a Hollywood studio.

Both **"Lucky"** and **"Chances"** were written and adapted for NBC television by Jackie, who also executive produced the highly successful six-hour miniseries **Lucky/Chances**, starring Nicollette Sheridan and Sandra Bullock.

In the nineties, she produced and wrote the four-hour miniseries, **Lady Boss**, which became another huge ratings success for NBC. **Lady Boss** starred Kim Delaney.

Next came **"American Star,"** a love story, which the Los Angeles Times described as **"classic Collins."**

Then the dangerously close to the truth **"Hollywood Kids"** – a story of power, sex, danger and ambition among the grown offspring of major celebrities.

In 1996 **"Vendetta – Lucky's Revenge"** was published – and became an immediate **New York Times** bestseller.

And in 1998, Jackie hosted her own daily television show for CBS, **Jackie Collins' Hollywood**. A combination of fun, style and interviews, Jackie talked to everyone from George Clooney to Jennifer Lopez.

After that she wrote **"L.A. Connections"** – a four-part serial novel published one per month – **"Power," "Obsession," "Murder"** and**"Revenge."**

In 1999 came **"Dangerous Kiss"** – the return of Lucky Santangelo in a bestselling novel about relationships, addiction, fear and lust.

In the year 2000, **"Lethal Seduction"** became the first bestseller for Jackie Collins in the new millennium. This tale of erotic suspense and glamorous intrigue featured Madison Castelli, a character first introduced in the **"L.A. Connections"** series.

"Hollywood Wives – The New Generation" became a blockbuster bestseller in 2001, following in the footsteps of the original**"Hollywood Wives." "Hollywood Wives – The New Generation"**featured a brand new cast of characters and a totally fresh perspective on how women pursue power, love, sex, and success in Tinseltown today.

In 2003 Jackie produced the TV movie of **"Hollywood Wives – The New Generation"** for CBS. **Wives** starred Farrah Fawcett, Robin Givens, Jack Scalia and Melissa Gilbert.

In June 2002, New York flash, L.A. trash and a Mafia don meet head-on in **"Deadly Embrace."** This sexy tale of dangerous passion and suspense features heroine Madison Castelli and is both a prequel and a sequel to her adventures in the bestselling **"Lethal Seduction."**

In 2003 came another **New York Times** bestseller, **"Hollywood Divorces,"** the story of three very different women. Followed in 2005 by **"Lovers and Players"** – a story of family conflicts, three brothers and their billionaire father, a beautiful heiress, a hip-hop mogul, Russian call girls, illegitimate children and two murders. This all takes place over seven days in New York, and yet again hit the **New York Times** bestseller list.

"Drop Dead Beautiful – The Continuing Adventures of Lucky Santangelo" was published in 2007. Lucky came back with a vengeance – bolder and more beautiful than ever! In **"Drop Dead Beautiful"** Lucky meets old friends and enemies, and deals with her wild teenage daughter, Max, who is as stubborn and strong as her mom. Lucky plans to return to Las Vegas and build an amazing billion-dollar hotel complex. But when she does… the trouble really begins…

Next came **"Married Lovers,"** a powerful look at the ins and outs of marriage in L.A. It's also the story of an under-age Russian girl who becomes involved in the sex trade, and eventually arrives in Hollywood and causes major trouble.

"Poor Little Bitch Girl" followed **"Married Lovers,"** another **New York Times** bestseller. It is the story of three very different women who all went to high school together. Denver Jones – a twenty-five-year-old kick-ass associate lawyer in L.A. Carolyn Henderson – assistant to a powerful married Senator in Washington. And Annabelle Maestro – daughter of movie star parents, who has carved out a niche for herself as a much-in-demand New York madame running call girls.

And then there is Bobby Santangelo – Lucky's Kennedyesque hot sexy son, with mucho style, great looks and plenty of money. Everyone wants Bobby…

Throw into this mix a raunchy agent, a sixteen-year-old gangbanger's girlfriend, an older superstar on the prowl, a lethal murder… and **"Poor Little Bitch Girl"** becomes a guilty pleasure for everyone to enjoy.

Jackie's next novel, **"Goddess of Vengeance,"** is the continuing adventures of Lucky Santangelo – much beloved by Jackie's legion of fans – who makes a triumphant return in this story of lust, power and revenge set between Los Angeles and Las Vegas. **The Daily Mail** called **"Goddess of Vengeance"** "the book of the year." Also returning in **"Goddess of Vengeance"** are Lucky's gorgeous son, Bobby, with his girlfriend, Denver, and Max, Lucky's wild little teenage daughter. And along for the thrilling ride is Armand Jordan, and to quote Jackie – "Armand is the nastiest villain I have ever created. But he was fun to write!"

And now comes a sexy sun-drenched thriller, **"The Power Trip,"** set on state of the art luxury yacht off the coast of Cabo San Luca. A tropical getaway with a cast of global power brokers and celebrities.

In **"The Power Trip"** you will meet Aleksandr Kasianenko, a billionaire Russian oligarch, as he sets sail on *The Bianca* with his sexy supermodel girlfriend, whom *The Bianca* is named after. Also five dynamic, powerful and famous couples invited on the yacht's maiden voyage: Hammond Patterson, a driven Senator, and his lovely but unhappy wife, Sierra. Cliff Baxter, a charming, never married movie star, and his ex-waitress girlfriend, Lori. Taye Sherwin, a famous black UK footballer and his interior designer wife, Ashley. Luca Perez, a male Latin singing sensation with his older decadent English boyfriend, Jeromy. And Flynn, a maverick journalist, with his Asian renegade female friend, Xuan.

You will also meet Russian mobster, Sergei Zukov, a man with a grudge against Aleksandr. And Sergei's Mexican beauty queen girlfriend, Ina, whose brother, Cruz, is a master pirate with orders to hold *The Bianca* and its illustrious rota of guests for ransom.

"The Power Trip" explores the decadent playgrounds of the super rich… and leaves you hungry for more. Take it if you dare…

Jackie recently completed work on a play – **"Hollywood Lies."** She is currently writing two new novels **"The Santangelos,"** and **"Wild Child,"** – a book about young Lucky. And also **"The Lucky Santangelo Cookbook – An Italian Feast."** Jackie is also working on a memoir, **"Reform School or Hollywood,"** and a coffee table book, **"Hollywood Snaps,"** filled with celebrity photos she has taken over the years.

Jackie lives in L.A. and calls herself a popular culture junkie. Her hobbies are music – everything from soul to rap, taking photographs, and visiting exotic locations so that she can write about them later.

Jackie firmly believes that the truth is always much stranger than fiction.

For A Quirky Fun Read,
Jackie Recommends...

"I found myself so deeply rooted into the lives of these characters
and could not put this book down until I read it all!"
- Kristi. Reading is
my Time Out blog

"This magical book truly is a must read. If you liked Bridget Jones
then you will love this. It has all the elements of a wonderfully feel
good romance intertwined with quirky and delightful characters
that we feel hugely invested in by the end of the book."
- M. Shine

Playing Along
A Novel By Rory Samantha Green

BUY IT NOW   FREE CHAPTER

Two Lives. Two Continents. One Song...

Then: George Bryce was an awkward, English schoolboy fantasizing about being in a band.

Now: George is front man of Thesis, an overnight indie scene sensation. Intense, creative and self-deprecating, his childhood dreams have all been fulfilled – so why does George still feel so lost?

Then: Lexi Jacobs was a confident Californian high school cheerleader, planning her future - marriage and a meaningful career.

Now: Lexi is searching for substance in a life full of mishaps. Cautious, bemused and rapidly losing the control she used to rely on, none of her teenage dreams have delivered and she's left wondering, "What next?"

Follow George and Lexi as they navigate their days thousands of miles apart. Fly with them from London to LA and back again, as George copes with the dynamics of his tight knit band and loose knit family, while Lexi juggles her eccentric new boss, bored best friend and smother mother.

Even though there's an ocean between them and their worlds couldn't be further apart, George and Lexi are pulled together through music, and their paths appear determined to cross.

The question is – when?

At the end of this delightfully quirky, irresistible story, you too will be left wondering which of your fantasies are destined to come true...

A Sexy, Sun-drenched New Thriller from Jackie Collins...

THE POWER TRIP

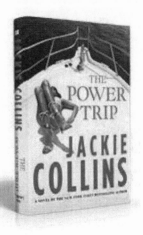

A tropical getaway with a cast of global power-hungry elites turns sour when they find out maybe they don't control as much of the world as they thought...

"Thrilling, sexy and totally compulsive. ★★★★★"
- Heat World

"Forget 50 Shades of Gray... Jackie Collins is 50 shades of FAB!
- OK! Magazine

A Russian billionaire and his state-of-the-art yacht. His beautiful and sexy supermodel girlfriend. And five dynamic, powerful and famous couples invited on the yacht's maiden voyage...

- ➤ A senator and his lovely but unhappy wife.
- ➤ A very attractive movie star and his needy ex-waitress girlfriend.
- ➤ A famous black footballer and his interior designer wife.
- ➤ A male Latin singing sensation and his older English boyfriend.
- ➤ And a maverick writer with his Asian journalist female friend.

Could this be the trip of a lifetime? Or a trip from hell? Whatever happens on the high seas doesn't *necessarily* stay there. The Power Trip – take it if you dare.

Made in the USA
San Bernardino, CA
21 August 2013